DEMIGODS ACADEMY

YEAR THREE

ELISA S. AMORE

KIERA LEGEND

DEMIGODS ACADEMY

CHAPTER ONE

MELANY

*a*s we crouched on the dirt and rocks on the edge of the gorge, the air around Lucian and me prickled on my skin as I unconsciously pulled the darkness closer, concealing us from the others. I heard Jasmine and Ren's voices calling out to me, but they eventually faded to silence.

Frantic, I looked around grasping for something in the shadows to make it better, to make Lucian better. I could no longer feel the heat of his body as I held him in my lap. His beautiful blue eyes, black pupils dilated, stared vacantly up into mine.

"You can't leave me." I leaned down and brushed my lips against his. They were cool, turning blue with every passing second that I couldn't help him. "I won't let you go," I murmured.

Tears poured down my cheeks. I was powerless to stop them. They streamed along my neck and dripped onto Lucian like spring raindrops. If only they were raindrops and could awaken him with their life-giving force. But nothing in this world was that just.

I gathered him in my arms, pulling him up to my chest, and buried my face in the side of his neck. I inhaled his scent of pine and sunshine, knowing it would be replaced with death and decay.

It wasn't fair that he was being taken. I'd done everything I was told to do. I followed the orders; I did what was expected of me. So why was I being punished like this? I could rally against the Gods for the injustice of it all, but I knew they wouldn't care. We were instruments to them, to be used for their purposes, playthings and pets, at best, to be coddled and prettied up when trotted out to the public. Just like Hades had done to me.

I hated them all for this. Lucian's death wouldn't go unanswered. Someone was going to pay for it. I made the vow deep in my soul, sealing it with the tornado of pain and rage inside me.

Gently, I lowered Lucian's body back to my lap. I kissed his lips, his cheeks, his brow. His eyes were still open, staring into nothingness. With the tips of my fingers, I closed them, leaving red prints on his lids. Tears still trickled down my cheeks, and I wiped at them with blood-stained hands.

I felt the weight of the dark amulet hanging around my neck as I shifted position. It was hot against my skin. I reached up and wrapped my bloody hand around it. I closed my eyes and whispered into the darkness.

"Take me instead."

The air instantly chilled, and I shivered. The shadows surrounding me began to move, swirling around like ink in water. The rushing sound of wings flapping echoed all around. I looked up to see a dark form with giant black wings hovering above me, then slowly lowering to the ground. At first, I thought it was Hades coming to take me back to the underworld, but the closer it got I realized how wrong I was.

Draped in a black shroud and carrying a long heavy-looking silver scythe, the tall figure drew near. Then it looked down at me with no face. Only darkness filled the space under the hood. It spoke, its voice a harsh and raspy buzzing in my ears.

"Do you wish to trade places with the fallen one?"

Before I could respond, another figure appeared in the sky also flapping large black wings. Hades landed beside the shrouded figure.

"She's not for you, Thanatos," he said.

"She summoned me."

Hades made a face. "No, she didn't. She summoned me. You were just looking for an excuse to take her."

Thanatos pointed a skeletal finger at Lucian. "I will take him then."

Hades sighed. "Not today."

Thanatos roared, his voice echoing painfully in my ears. "You cannot have both."

"I can and I will."

"You will pay for this Hades."

Hades nodded. "Whatever."

Thanatos roared again, then he exploded into a million black feathers. They drifted down to the ground and on top of my head. I swiped at them and frowned up at Hades.

"I didn't summon you."

"You did with your tears."

He crouched next to me and reached for Lucian. I held onto him. "What are you doing?"

"Just give him to me."

My heart leapt into my throat as I slapped at his grasping hands. "No! You can't take him from me!" I burst into uncontrollable sobs, not caring that tears gushed from my eyes and my nose ran.

He looked at me for a long moment, his face softened. He lifted a hand and touched the tears on my cheeks. "Your pain is powerful. I can feel it inside."

"He's dead and it's my fault." I looked up at Hades, pleading for him to do something to take my pain away. I didn't care how he did it. I just wanted to be free of it. He should have let Thanatos claim me.

He reached for Lucian again. "Just give him to me before I can't do anything for him."

I relinquished my hold on Lucian, and Hades gathered him in his arms. He closed his eyes and pressed the palms of his hands down onto Lucian's chest. At first nothing happened, then a dark purple glow emanated from Hades's hands and slowly enveloped Lucian's body until he too glowed like amethyst.

The hair on the back of my neck rose as I watched Hades pour dark energy into Lucian. A prickling sensation whispered over my scalp and then down my arms until it crept throughout my body, making me shiver. I didn't know what to expect from this. How could a person be brought back from death? It was a type of magic I was unfamiliar with. I held my breath, eyeing Lucian's body for any twitch or flinch, any indication that it was working.

Hades's eyes snapped open, and he scowled. He looked down at Lucian's body, and I saw the confusion in his face. "It's not working."

I shook my head. "Keep trying. Please!"

"He's too far gone. His soul has already left his body."

"No! I won't accept that." I leaned forward and placed my hands down on top of Hades's. I closed my eyes and pushed everything I had forward. Every spark of energy, every flicker of flame, every molecule of water, every speck of earth, every tendril of shadow. Every aspect of who I was, I forced through my body and out of my hands and into Hades.

I opened my eyes as I heard Lucian's small gasp and watched as his face contorted. Was it in pain or something else? I couldn't tell. The purple glow grew brighter. I had to squint to look at Lucian. And then I saw it. The rise of Lucian's chest. His mouth opened and he sucked in air. Hades fell back, the dark glow shattering like purple glass, shards of it sprinkled onto the ground around us. Then Lucian took in another breath, then another.

I touched his face. His skin was cool and clammy but warming under my fingers. "Lucian?"

I could see his eyes moving around, then slowly, they opened, and his gaze fixed on me. He blinked several times, then licked his lips. "What...what happened?"

Smiling, I leaned down and pressed my lips to his brow, then I looked up as Hades got to his feet, brushing at the dirt on his black pants as if he'd not just brought back a person from the dead.

"Hades, I—,"

He waved his hand toward me. "I'll see you later in the hall." Then he turned and stepped into the darkest part of the shadows still surrounding us and disappeared. The moment he vanished, the darkness fell away.

Jasmine, Ren, and the others who had gathered around the injured firefighters ran toward us.

"What happened?" Jasmine demanded. "You just disappeared."

Ren's eyes grew wide as he spotted Lucian sitting up and rubbing at his face. "How...but he was..."

"Hades saved him," I blurted in a rush of laughing and crying at the same time. My emotions were so conflicted that it felt like one big ball of chaotic energy inside my belly.

Ren helped Lucian to his feet, then he turned him around to look at his back. His shirt was torn away and bloody, but his back was clear of any wound. The only marks were from where his wings emerged. "It's like you never got stung."

Lucian rubbed his head again. "I have the worst headache." His knees buckled, and he would've fallen again if it hadn't been for me and Ren grabbing hold of his arms and body.

"You need to go to the infirmary," Jasmine said.

Lucian nodded.

I put my arm around his waist to support him then looked around, noticing the glaring absence of the dead chimera that was supposed to be on the ground. "Where's the chimera?"

"The Furies took the body away." Jasmine grimaced. "They said they had a use for its parts."

I didn't even want to think about what the sisters would use the chimera for. I pushed it out of my mind as I considered the best way to get Lucian back to the academy and to the infirmary where Chiron could look him over. There was no way he could fly. We'd have to go my way. Although I was positive none of my friends were going to be comfortable with it.

"Where's Georgina and the rest of crew?" I asked.

"They've already been evacuated," Jasmine said.

"Okay, everyone, gather around me. I'm going to take us back to the academy."

"How are you going to do that?" Ren narrowed his eyes at me.

"You'll have to trust me."

As everyone looked sideways at me, I wasn't sure they trusted me entirely. That hurt a bit, but it couldn't be helped. And I wasn't about to beg them to.

Jasmine and Marek moved in closer to me, Lucian, and Ren, who was still helping Lucian stand. When everyone was grouped closely, I sent out feelers toward the nearest shadows. They were hard to find in the bright sunlight, but eventually I caught onto a few near the treeline and drew them toward me. After a few more minutes, we were covered in darkness.

"Follow me." I stepped forward into the dimmest part of the shadows. I could sense the others' hesitation, but eventually they did what I asked, and we all sunk into the black abyss. A few seconds later, I led them out of the darkness, and we emerged into the corridor just outside the infirmary.

Ren and I half-carried/half-dragged Lucian inside. Chiron turned to see us come in and shook his head. "Now what?"

"Lucian was stung by a chimera's snake tail," I said. "He...he died."

Chiron's eyes narrowed as he looked from to Lucian then back to me again. "He doesn't look dead."

"Hades healed him."

Chiron's eyes widened as he gaped at me. Then he took Lucian from us and lay him down on one of the cots. "Okay, you got my attention. In two thousand years, I've known of only one other person that Hades ever brought back from the dead. You're a lucky guy."

As Chiron started his poking and prodding at Lucian, he pointed to the door and told us to leave.

I didn't want to go. I'd lost Lucian, and I felt like if I walked through that door, I'd never see him again.

Jasmine put her hand on my arm and guided me out. "He'll be okay. He's safe now."

Once we were outside in the hall, I could feel my anger building again. The chimera had been released on purpose. Its intent was to kill as many of us as possible. I had no doubts about that in my mind. And I knew who released it—Aphrodite.

If she wanted a war, she was going to get one.

Without a word, I stepped into the nearest shadow to find out exactly where she was so we could have a little chat about that.

CHAPTER TWO

MELANY

I emerged from the shadows just outside of the tall golden doors leading to Aphrodite's Hall. I grabbed the door handle, twisted it, and threw the door open. I was surprised it didn't bang against the wall. Marching inside, I was fully aware of how I must've looked in my battle gear with arms and hands stained with Lucian's blood. A couple of people leapt out of my way, with looks of fear and terror, as I whirled down the hall like a black and red tornado.

At first, I wasn't sure Aphrodite was in the hall, but then I heard her shrill laugh through the open door of the side rooms. I entered to see the Goddess holding court. She lounged on one of the white sofas that were synonymous with her gilded hall, her long golden dress draped over the edge. She had a glass of red wine in one hand and a bunch of grapes in the other. She looked like one of her paintings that plastered the walls.

Her sculpted eyebrows went up when she spotted me. "Melany. How delightful. We were just discussing the success the academy had fighting the forest blaze. Well done, you."

Those who had been sitting on the floor in rapture of her—Revana among them—stood as I stomped toward Aphrodite. The Goddess didn't bother to rise. She was obviously very comfortable right where she was. She gave nothing away. I wasn't surprised. She'd had thousands of years to perfect the art of denial and Machiavellian schemes.

"We were successful. No thanks to you," I said, my voice low and growly.

Her gaze raked over me. "Is there a reason you're in my hall covered in blood? It's quite disgusting."

"This blood is on your hands."

"How so? I've been here the entire time." She took a sip of her wine and popped a grape into her mouth.

The others in the hall were getting quite a show, their heads turned from Aphrodite to me, to her again with each verbal volley.

"We encountered a chimera in the forest. A chimera you released to start the fire."

She made a face, feigning shock. "A chimera? How awful. Was anyone hurt?"

"A couple firefighters died, burned to death, and Lucian…"

Revana stepped forward. "Lucian's hurt?"

I didn't look at her. I just kept my gaze on Aphrodite. "He died. Stung by the chimera. And it's your fault." I pointed at her.

This time she got to her feet. Slowly, lazily, as if I wasn't accusing her of killing people and had just come for a social visit.

"Lucian's dead?" Revana moved toward me. Her hands were clenched at her sides, although I sensed that if she could have gotten away with it, she'd have used those hands on me.

"Hades healed him." I looked at Revana. I knew she had feelings for Lucian, so I threw her a bone. "He's in the infirmary."

Aphrodite moved toward me. It was so smooth and effortless. It looked like she was floating. "I'm offended that you'd come into my hall and accuse me of releasing a monstrous creature into the world." She stood right in front of me with a snide smile just dripping with venom. "What proof do you have?"

"I heard you and Ares conspiring."

She rolled her eyes. "Didn't we already go over this with Zeus? You already accused me of conspiring, and it got you nowhere. Zeus didn't believe you and rightly so."

"Zeus is blind to your treachery."

"Careful now." She ran her finger over the rim of the wineglass in her hand. "Saying such things about the all-powerful could get you into some serious trouble."

I met her gaze with my own spitefulness. "I know what you did. I know that you and your lover Ares are planning something." I spoke the word lover with such rancor it left a sour taste in my mouth.

Her eyes flashed with fire, and she leaned down to me. I could smell the wine on her breath. We were so close. I could see the gold flecks in her eyes glow with power. "The only reason I don't reach into your mouth right now and rip out your heart is because you're Hades's little pet. And he is sentimentally attached to his pets. I mean, he lets that dog of his run loose sometimes." She straightened and took a step back, turning away from me. "Revana, please escort Melany out of this hall. I'm tired of her silly false allegations. They're boring me."

Revana looked from Aphrodite to me. I could see some hesitation in her face. Was she hesitating because she was afraid of me or her Goddess? Eventually, her misplaced loyalty won out, and she nodded toward the door, her eyes narrowed with a fierce intensity.

"Time to go."

I didn't move. I came for a fight, and I wasn't leaving without one.

Revana reached out to grab my arm to guide me to the exit. It was a mistake on her part as I was ramped up for any kind of fight.

Lightning quick I wrapped my hand around her wrist and twisted her arm around until I could've easily broken it with just a bit more well-placed pressure. She tried to break free, but every movement she made just put more strain on her arm, and she winced from the pain I imagined zipped up to her shoulder.

"Aphrodite is lying to you, Revana. She doesn't give one shit about you, or any of her disciples. You're playthings to her. Like dolls manipulated for her amusement."

"She's just rambling." Aphrodite waved her hand toward me. "Everyone knows she's gone crazy. That's what happens to girls when they go to Hades's Hall. All those months down in the underworld with no one to talk to. It would drive anyone mad."

"I'm not crazy," I hissed at her.

"Oh, my dear, you have no idea what he's turned you into. He did it to poor Persephone and now to you. I'd feel sorry for you if you weren't pissing me off so badly with your lies about me and Ares."

Hearing the name Persephone gave me pause, and I relinquished my hold on Revana's arm. She stepped away from me and rubbed at her wrist and forearm.

"What happened to her? To Persephone?"

Aphrodite's grin sent a shiver down my spine. "She went crazy, tried to leave the underworld, but Hades wouldn't let her. Zeus had to intervene to save her life. If you're not careful, the same thing is going to happen to you." She flicked her hand toward me. "Now leave. My patience is wearing thin, and I won't be held responsible for what could happen next."

I wasn't afraid of her, or what she could do to me.

I'd already survived one attempt on my life when she tried to squeeze me to death while she was a snake, but I wasn't going to gain the upper hand this way. I had to get proof of her treachery and expose her in front of the whole academy. If I went to Zeus again, he could just sweep it under the rug as if it never happened.

"This isn't over."

Aphrodite chuckled. "Do get some sleep, Melany. You look beyond ragged."

I marched out of the room and back toward the main doors. Revana was right on my tail. I could've told her she didn't have to escort me, that I knew the way. Right before I left, she grabbed my arm and spun me around.

"Is Lucian really okay?"

My first inclination was to grab her hand and crush it in mine, but the look on her face wasn't one of confrontation but of concern and worry. It cracked through my fury and seeped through to my core. Our feelings for Lucian were the only thing that united us.

I nodded. "He is now. He died in my arms, until Hades brought him back from the dead. He's in the infirmary if you want to see him."

She let her hand drop from my arm. She seemed almost sheepish for grabbing it in the first place.

"I know you don't believe me, but Aphrodite is not your friend. She's dangerous."

Revana's eyebrow lifted. "She says the same about you."

"Well, she'd be right." I turned and walked away, finding a shadow to dissolve into to travel back to the infirmary.

Before I stepped out of the darkness, I heard Jasmine and Georgina talking just outside the infirmary doors.

"You should've seen her, Gina. She was magnificent but terrifying." Jasmine shook her head. "I'd never seen anyone fight like that. I was just happy that we were fighting on the same side."

"She's still Melany. She's still our friend."

"Is she? I don't know. It feels like she has her own agenda that has nothing to do with us. When she came out of the dark riding Cerberus with the Furies at her side…" She sighed and shook her head again. "My whole body shook in fear. I don't know. Maybe I'm just tired and being overly sensitive."

Georgina put her hand on Jasmine's shoulder. "You should go back to your dorm and sleep. We all should. What we did today was good, Jas. We saved lives."

"I know, I just wish I wasn't afraid of Mel. Maybe I'm just afraid for her. I saw how she was with Hades. There's a connection there, and that terrifies me."

"It scares me too."

I'd heard enough. I stepped out of the shadows right next to them. They both jumped.

"Mel? Where did you go? We were worried." Jasmine tried to reach out to me, but I avoided her touch.

"It's not me you need to worry about." I walked into the infirmary toward Lucian's bed. Chiron was there, and he crossed the room to intercept me.

"He needs his rest. Come back in a day or two when he might be up for visitors."

"Just tell me one thing: is he going to be okay?"

Chiron nodded. "Yes. I don't know exactly what Hades did to him or for him, but he'll have a full recovery."

"Thanks."

I left the infirmary, and Jasmine and Georgina ambushed me.

"Is Lucian going to be okay?"

"Yes."

"What exactly happened?" Jasmine asked.

"Hades brought him back from the dead."

"How?"

I shrugged. I didn't know how to answer her because I really didn't know myself. He'd said that he couldn't do it, and it wasn't until I laid my hands on his that Lucian started to breathe. I had done something but didn't know exactly what that was. Had I made some subconscious deal with Thanatos for Lucian's life? Or had I made that deal with Hades? Did he own me now?

I had to find out.

"I've got to go," I said as I started for the nearest dim corner.

"Can't you stay longer? Have dinner with us in the

dining hall like old times." Georgina eyes pleaded with me.

"The old times are gone, Gina." I moved toward the shadows. The second my boot touched the darkness, I wrapped my hand around the dark amulet at my throat and was immediately sucked into the abyss.

CHAPTER THREE

MELANY

My entire body shook as I stepped out of the shadows and into Hades's Hall. I was running on pure adrenaline. But I needed answers and a long hot shower before I could even think about getting any amount of sleep.

I marched into the library to find Hades. He sat in one of the large chairs by the fire sipping an amber liquid in a short glass and reading a book. When I approached, he casually bookmarked his page with a thin red satin ribbon and set the book down on the table beside him. He arched an eyebrow at me.

"I take it this is going to be some long tirade." Before I could say anything, he stood and moved toward the table with the crystal decanters of water, wine, and other liquids. "Let me pour you a drink."

"I don't want a drink. I want some answers."

He poured me a drink anyway, the same amber liquid that was in his glass. He offered it to me. I grabbed the glass and took a sip. It was strong and burned in my throat, but it warmed my belly the moment it hit, chasing away the exhaustion. I took another drink and drained it in one gulp, then set the glass down on the table with a loud clink.

"Why did you save Lucian?"

Hades shrugged. "It seemed like his death would've been a waste of a good fighter."

"Bullshit. I don't believe you."

"Believe what you want, girl, it's of no consequence to me." He tried to move away from me, but I stepped in his path. His gaze narrowed intensely as he stared down at me.

"You did it for me, didn't you?"

His lips twitched into a wry condescending smirk. "Your schoolgirl crush on me is flattering, Melany, but you really need to rein it in if I'm going to continue to teach you. I'd hate to relinquish my claim on you. You'd probably end up in Zeus's clan or, gasp, Hephaistos's. Talk about a waste."

He tried to go around me again, but I braced my hand against his chest. He looked down at it then back at my face. His eyes narrowed, darkening to pitch. It was now or never. With adrenaline still pumping through me along with the alcohol I'd just consumed, I fisted my hand in his shirt, perched on my tiptoes, and kissed him.

At first, I thought he was going to succumb to me and deepen the kiss, but when it was over and I naturally pulled back, licking my lips where a jolt of electricity still sizzled, he had the nerve to tilt his head indulgently and pat me on the head.

"Run along, Melany. You had a long emotional day and you clearly need some sleep."

"Argh! You're an asshole!" I stomped out of the library, across the hall to my room. Once inside, I slammed the door shut, locked it and cursed a blue streak all the way into the bathroom.

I stripped off my dirty clothes and stepped into the huge glassed-in shower stall. When I turned on the hot water tap, I was instantly hit with a hard spray from overhead and from the sides. I stood there, my face lifted to the scalding water, and let it wash away the conflicted emotions that were assaulting me.

Anger and fury mixed with grief and longing. I supposed those feelings were connected in various ways. I just didn't know how I felt at that moment. Anger still rippled inside me from having been forced to deal with the chimera while trying to save lives. I could still hear the screams of the firefighters as they were burned alive from the monster's fire. I was still grieving for Lucian's loss while trying to grasp onto the relief and joy that his return from the dead should have filled me with.

Then there were the emotions for Hades swirling around inside me making things very difficult and uncomfortable. Those confused me the most. I was angry at him for being so arrogant and superior all the time and grateful to him for healing Lucian and bringing him back to me. I burned so hard for him it was almost painful.

It was that last one that gave me the most trouble. I couldn't desire Hades. It was wrong on so many levels. He was my teacher, my mentor, an arrogant jerk, a dangerous God. He wasn't nice or thoughtful or caring like Lucian. But I wanted Hades anyway. That probably said more about me than it did about him.

After I finished washing and rinsing, I turned off the tap, opened the door and reached for the towel on the heated rack, thankful for the warming sensation on my body. I dried off, slid on the black fuzzy robe that I'd been given when I first got here, and walked out of the bathroom fully intending to climb into bed and sleep.

I pulled up short, stunned, when I spotted Hades sitting stiffly on the edge of my bed.

When he stood, my racing heart leapt into my throat and butterflies fluttered deep in my belly. I didn't know what to do as he moved toward me, his gaze everywhere but on me. For the briefest moment, the word RUN screamed in my head, but I didn't move. I couldn't. And honestly, I didn't want to.

He stopped a mere foot in front of me and lifted his gaze to mine. I couldn't stop the flustered gasp that sprung my lips.

"You're playing with fire, girl. You know that, don't you?"

"Yes." My voice was raspy, thick with desire.

He took a step forward, and I took one back. "I'm not some boy you can tease and taunt." His gaze raked me from head to toe. The tip of his tongue poked out to wet his lips.

"I know." The ache in my belly deepened. I nearly groaned as every muscle in my body quickened in anticipation of what I hoped he'd do to me. I had a very vivid imagination.

"If you truly knew, you'd run as far and fast as you could go." He closed the small distance between us, as my back hit the wall. He dipped his head, so his lips were mere inches from mine. "Beg me to take you, and I'll fulfil every desire you've ever had."

I pressed my lips together, then whispered, "Please. I want you—,"

His hands dove into my hair and his lips were on mine. He kissed me until my head swam. All I could think about was him pressed against my body, the heat he gave off, the scent of his cologne, and the taste of him on my lips. Everything about him was fire and passion, and I was a match just waiting to be struck and burned.

Then he pulled back, his eyes lowering to the tie on my robe. He reached out and slowly undid it. I swallowed as the robe parted just enough to show a sliver of my body. Licking his lips, Hades kept my gaze, then he took the two edges of the robe, eased them apart and slowly pushed the robe over my shoulders.

I stood there, fully naked, exposed, vulnerable, my

entire body quivering as he stared at me. His gaze was hot and hungry, and I wanted to slap my hands over my breasts and between my legs, but he gripped my arms and pressed them against the wall so I couldn't. I took in a ragged breath and gnawed at my bottom lip with my teeth, so I wouldn't cry out from frustration and desperation. I needed him to touch me; I was sure I'd wither away to dust if he didn't.

Finally, blissfully, he kissed me again. He pressed his body against mine, the fabric of his suit rubbed over the sensitive tips of my breasts, and I could feel how much he wanted me. There was no mistaking it, and I was empowered to know I could do that to him.

When he pulled back again, I mewled in protest. His lips twitched into a sly smile, then he moved away from me, letting his hold on my arms drop. I was about to tell him to stop, when he slid off his jacket, then unbuttoned his shirt.

When he was shirtless, I admired the cut of his pecs and the ridges along his flat stomach. His skin was pale and smooth like marble except for a thin line of dark hair that led to the band of his trousers, which he was undoing. He looked as strong and fierce as I knew he would be. He was a God and a gorgeous one at that.

He stripped his pants off; the rest of him was as hard and beautiful. Then he moved toward me again, predator-like. I was both excited and scared. I couldn't stop shaking. I'd had sex before, but this was beyond anything I'd ever experienced. Hades was beyond any man. Was I truly ready for this?

Pressing up against me, his lips nibbled on the side of my neck while his hand slid up to my breast, caressing it with his fingers playing over the sensitive tip. I let out a long low groan. He trailed his tongue and teeth along my jawline and over my mouth. A hand dipped down over my hip, then he pulled up my leg, hooking it up over his waist.

Gasping, I bowed my back as he entered me. Although I was ready for him, he had to go slow. He gritted his teeth; the muscles along his jawline clenched. I knew he wanted to thrust into me but restrained himself so he wouldn't hurt me. When he was finally seated inside me, he kissed me again, his tongue dipping inside my mouth, and started to move.

I dug my fingers into his back and held on as he took me beyond the limits of pleasure.

At first, we were screwing up against the wall, the rough texture of the stone wall scraping along my skin. Then, we were on top of a large bed with black silk sheets. I could feel the satin caressing my backside as Hades thrust into me again and again.

We weren't in my room though, or Hades's room, but a vast rock cavern, a large fire with flames as high as the stone ceiling crackling nearby. Our bodies were slick with sweat, the glow of the fire cocooning us in orange and red. The place matched how I felt inside.

I grabbed onto him, one hand in his hair the other on his ass, as his strokes became harder and faster. Every muscle in my body clenched and quaked. My heart raced so fast I could barely breathe as my body was pushed to the edge of bliss.

With one final deep thrust, Hades cried out in a language I didn't understand.

My entire body convulsed as an orgasm rippled through me. "Oh, Gods!"

Light burst behind my eyes, as sound roared in my ears. I bowed my back and crushed him around the waist with my thighs as every nerve in my body snapped. I was a swirling tsunami of sensation as I came. I bucked against it, both pushing and pulling Hades, as he continued to coax more pleasure out of me with every slight movement of his body inside mine.

He nuzzled his face into the side of my neck. He licked me, then his mouth covered mine and he kissed me until both our bodies stopped quaking. Panting hard, he peppered kisses along my chin and neck, then he rolled off me and onto his back onto the bed.

I blinked up at the canopy overhead and realized we were back inside my room. I turned my head to look at him. His eyes were closed, and he had an arm flung up over his head. I watched the quick rise and fall of his chest. Hesitant, I reached over and touched him, making sure that this had been real and not a dream.

He covered my hand with his own then opened his eyes and looked at me. I wasn't sure what I saw in those dark depths. I wanted to believe there was affection there; I'd felt it as he made love to me. I wasn't a fool to think there was love. I didn't know if he could even feel that way about anyone.

But for one moment, I fantasized that he felt it about me as I felt it for him.

Hades sat up briefly to pull up the blanket to cover us both. Then he pulled me up onto his chest and brushed his fingers through my hair until we both fell into a blissful deep sleep.

CHAPTER FOUR

LUCIAN

I dreamt of fire.

I was running through a cave, and flames flickered along the stone walls bathing everything in red and orange. Behind me, running just as fast, loped a large black beast with teeth as long as my forearm and breath that stunk of brimstone and ash.

As I sprinted over the rough, uneven rock floor seemingly for my life, all I could think about was Melany. She was here somewhere in the cave, and I had to get to her before the beast consumed her alive.

Sweat coated my body as I ran, my arms and legs pumping mercilessly. My lungs burned, and my heart throbbed from the effort. I could hear screams all around me. Female screams. Melany's screams. But at one point, I wasn't one hundred percent sure if they were cries of pain or agony or of extreme pleasure.

That made it worse and sent sickly shivers up and down my spine.

I kept running, glancing over my shoulder to see how close the beast was getting. That had been a mistake, and I tripped over a stubby protruding stalagmite. I fell to my knees onto the hard, rocky surface, pain shot up my legs from the impact. A thick dark shadow crawled over me, and I knew I was doomed.

I flipped over as Cerberus cornered me, three sets of glowing red eyes glaring at me. He snorted and smoke curled out of his nostrils. But the worse part was the man who had been riding the hound. Hades slid off the beast's back and loomed over me like a dark specter.

He smiled, and I felt like a knife slid between my ribs and into my heart. "Don't worry, boy, I can't kill you. I'm a part of you now."

"Where's Melany?" I demanded with more bravado then I felt.

"Can't you tell by her screams? She's with me. In the underworld. In my bed."

His words made me nauseous, and I felt like I was going to retch. I scrambled away from him and got back onto my feet. "I don't believe you."

"Yes, you do. You knew this day was coming. You sensed the changes in her. You knew she was no longer the girl that awkwardly stumbled into the academy with a stolen shadowbox." He looked amused, and it made my stomach roil. "You saw how she looked at me. Hungry for the darkness."

I shook my head. "I don't care what you say. She'll never be yours."

"She already is." Hades swirled his hand in the air, and the shadows curled around him like a black opaque curtain. Within those shades I saw Melany with her arms around Hades. She turned her head ever so slightly toward me, and she was laughing.

I jolted out of the darkness. I didn't quite wake up but was floating in the space between sleep and consciousness. It was pleasant, warm and non-threatening. Safe. Then I heard voices nearby. I couldn't tell who they belonged to, or whether they were male or female even.

"The girl knows too much. I suspect Hades is feeding her all kinds of stories."

"She won't know what is truth or fiction."

"Some will listen to her. She has supporters in the academy. Not only students but professors."

"She needs to die."

"We can't get to her. She's under Hades's protection."

"We have to get her out into the open."

"She'll be guarded in a battle, like she was in the fire."

"Then it has to be during another event. Some place and time she won't expect."

"It has to be soon, before she finds out the truth about the academy and…"

The voices faded. I tried to focus my energy on getting them back, but it was too hard. Slowly my warm place was becoming cold and unwelcoming. I struggled inside that space, punching and kicking my way out, my way up to the surface.

Light pierced my eyelids, and I cracked one then the other open. Blinking away the drugged-sensation, I turned my head to survey my surroundings. I was in a bed in the infirmary. I turned my head again to see several faces looking down at me.

"Welcome back." Zeus smiled at me.

As did, Ares, Demeter, Dionysus, Aphrodite, Heracles, and Chiron who were all gathered around my bed.

"Chiron wasn't sure if you were going to come out of it so soon."

"We all heard about your heroic deeds and had to come down to see how you were doing." Aphrodite patted my hand.

I licked my lips which were dry and cracked. "What happened?"

While Chiron helped me sit up to drink some water, Dionysus gleefully said, "Well, you died. What did it feel like? Do you remember?"

Ares nudged him away. "Leave him alone. He's a great warrior. A hero."

I closed my eyes for a moment and remembered the pain that surged through me from the chimera's sting. I shuddered. I also remembered being on the ground in Melany's arms. After that, it was all a bit fuzzy. Hades had been there, I could feel his dark cold touch on my chest, and I remembered waking up and my friends helping me to my feet and coming here.

"Okay, time for everyone to leave," Chiron said. "Lucian needs his rest."

Zeus squeezed my shoulder. "When you are feeling better, son, the academy is going to host a grand ceremony for you and the others who battled the great fire and saved many lives. You are all heroes, and we're going to celebrate your bravery."

"Melany…"

Zeus nodded. "Oh yes, she will most definitely be invited."

"Hades…," I said, trailing off, unsure of what I wanted to say about him.

"We'll invite him, too. We'll make it so he can't say no." He gave me a little wink, as if we were sharing an inside joke. He leaned down closer to my ear. "I'm proud to have you as part of my clan, Lucian. One day I could see you leading my army."

He tipped his head to me, then followed the others out of the infirmary, leaving me with Chiron who forced a disgusting tincture down my throat claiming it would help me get my strength back. Then, he left me to rest.

But I couldn't rest. I had to find Melany and warn her. Someone was out to harm her, but I didn't know who. I could've easily assumed it was Ares and Aphrodite, as Melany had already accused them of treachery, but there had been others in the room. I wouldn't like to believe that Demeter, Dionysus, or

Heracles would want to hurt Melany. They were friends, but I couldn't be sure about anything anymore.

I sat up all the way. I had to stop and breathe deeply as a wave of nausea overtook me. Once it passed, I swung my legs over the edge of the bed, my feet touching the floor. That was then I noticed that I was dressed only in a hospital-like gown with no pants and no socks. I stood, felt faint, but moved past it. I looked around to find my clothes but didn't have any luck in finding them. I was going to have to do this as is.

I started across the room toward the exit when a searing burn zipped across my chest. I put my hand up to my sternum, but it hurt when I pressed there. I pulled down the neckline of the gown and spotted several dark purple marks on my chest.

I moved to the dressing mirror in the corner of the room near the sink. I yanked down the gown so I could fully see the bruises that marred my skin. There were several dark blotches. Some were small, the shape and size of a dime, others were inch-long streaks, then there was a large square-shaped bruise below the others. Frowning, I studied them in the mirror. My stomach roiled as I took a step back, and I could see that all the marks together made up the shape of a handprint.

It was Hades's hand that had healed me.

I thought about the dream I had. There were only remnants left in my mind, nothing was too clear. Only whispers of sensations and sounds. The echo of Melany's passionate screams still faintly buzzed in my ears. But I did recall Hades's words. "I can't kill you. I'm a part of you now."

If that was true, maybe then I could use that to travel to the underworld and find Melany.

I shuffled over to the dimmest area of the infirmary where the shadows seemed to gather as if in a meeting. Erebus had taught us how to hide inside the darkness, using it as camouflage, but maybe I could use it like Melany did to travel from here to Hades's Hall.

With my hand, I reached into the shadows and tried to pull them over me, the same way I'd seen Melany do it. At first, nothing happened. I was just grabbing at air. Then a chill enveloped me and slowly I became surrounded by the dark, the infirmary fading away to nothing.

"Now what?" I sighed, unsure of what to do next.

I thought about the trip to the underworld that Jasmine, Georgina, and I took, after I gave blood to that witch, Hecate. I pictured the river that we needed to cross, and the cave beyond that. Had that been the cave I'd encountered in my dream?

I concentrated on that river and that cave, then took a step forward. I thought for sure I was going to walk right into the wall of the infirmary with every small step I took, but I didn't. I sensed I wasn't in that room any longer but somewhere else. Some strange place between corporeal planes.

Still with that image in my mind, I kept walking in the hope that I wasn't just going to be lost in the shadowy spots for an eternity with no way back. I had to believe I was going to end up somewhere.

For what seemed like hours, I kept walking, putting one foot in front of the other, until finally I could hear the rush of water. Buoyed by the sound, I walked a bit faster. Then I felt cold wet stone on the bottom of my foot. The shadows dissolved and I was in the cave. In front of me, looming like a castle tower, were black stone doors.

I made it. I was at the doors to Hades's Hall.

I tried the door handle. It wouldn't turn, so I knocked. The sound echoed around me like thunder bouncing off the stone walls.

"Who's there?"

I whipped around toward the voice and saw Hades sitting atop his three-headed demon hound. I hadn't even heard them approach, which was insane considering the size of the beast. His paws were as big around as a kitchen table.

"Now you're supposed to say Lucian."

Cerberus dipped his head toward me—his nose was the size of my head—and took in a large whiff of me. I wondered if he just smelled his lunch special of the day.

"I need to see Melany," I said.

Hades jumped down from his hound and stepped toward me. "Why?"

"She's in danger. I have to warn her."

"About what?"

"Tell her not to come to the hero ceremony. It's a trap. Someone wants to kill her."

"Who? Zeus?"

I shook my head. "I don't know. I didn't see faces, just heard words about that fact that she knows too much and that they want to draw her out into the open."

Hades rubbed at his chin. "I suspected as much."

"It's your fault." I took a step toward him despite shaking inside. "You put her in danger."

Hades's gaze focused on me. It was direct and intense and sent a shiver down my spine. But I didn't back down like he wanted me to. I wouldn't. Not when it was Melany's life that balanced on the edge.

"I admire your courage to come down here, Lucian. I really do. But don't make the mistake of thinking I won't hurt you. I may not be able to kill you, but there are other inventive ways to inflict pain and suffering."

"I want to see Melany. She deserves to know."

"Oh, I'll tell her to be sure." He smiled. "But she's sleeping right now. All worn out, I'm afraid." That grin again that made my stomach roil. "I'm sure you can imagine why."

I thought about my dream again and realized maybe it hadn't exactly been one. Melany's cries of passion filled my mind again.

"You've done your duty. You've brought the warning now go back to the academy where you belong."

"You can't keep me from her forever." I lifted my head and kept his gaze.

"Oh, I can try." He reached out and pressed a finger against my chest. The burn was instant, and I went sailing backward into the darkness as if hit by a sledgehammer. Seconds later, I landed in a heap on the infirmary floor.

A lot more unsteady than before, I got to my feet and made it back to my cot. I drank more of the tincture that Chiron had made me, vowing that I would do whatever it took to get stronger because I knew without a shadow of a doubt that Melany was going to need me to protect her. Not only from those who would seek to harm her but from Hades. He posed the most danger.

CHAPTER FIVE

MELANY

*A*fter I woke, I lay in bed on my back and stared up at the canopy wondering if I had dreamt the whole thing. I lifted the covers to see I had my sleeping clothes on and that I wasn't still naked. I turned my head and looked at the other side of the bed, trying to picture Hades sleeping there. I ran my hand over the dark sheets. They were cold to the touch.

I touched my lips with my fingers. His taste still lingered there. I could still feel the electricity of our coupling all along my body. My muscles ached a little, especially the ones between my thighs. We most definitely had sex. I hadn't dreamt it. It had been real.

And so amazing.

The bell above my bed jangled, and I rolled out of bed. I got washed and changed and wandered down the hall to the dining room for breakfast. My belly flip-flopped in anticipation of seeing Hades. But he wasn't at the table. I was alone again for breakfast with only the little serving robot for company. I ate quickly then went down to the training room.

When I stepped inside, Megaera and Tisiphone were flying around in the air sparring with swords, and Allecto was throwing knives into the wooden training dummies in the corner. When they spotted me, Tisiphone clapped.

My cheeks flushed. I really hoped it wasn't because she knew I'd had sex with Hades. I would be mortified.

She drifted to the ground as did Megaera, then came over to me. "There she is. The mighty chimera slayer."

Relief surged over me, and I smiled and nodded. "Well, technically you three finished it off."

"True." Tisiphone unsheathed a dagger at her waist. "I made a blade out of the chimera's fangs. Isn't it cool?"

She handed it to me, and I made all the appropriate noises, then handed it back to her. I had to suppress a shudder to think she had actually removed its teeth and fashioned a weapon out of them. When Allecto joined us, I noticed she wore a new fur cape. I swallowed when I realized it was from the hide of the chimera.

She must've noticed my disdain because she said, "It honors the enemy and the battle when you create something new from their death."

I shuddered even more, thinking about what they

would make out of me, if we were ever on opposite sides of a battle and I lost to them. Would Allecto be wearing a Melany cape made from my pale skin and blue hair?

"We heard the golden-haired boy survived," Megaera said.

I nodded.

"That's good. He's a good fighter."

"And pretty to look at, too," Tisiphone added with a leer. "Does he belong to you?"

I frowned. "What do you mean?"

"Is he, you know, yours?"

"What she means is, are you two having sex?" Allecto interrupted.

"No."

"So, you won't mind if I indulge—,"

"I do mind, actually." I couldn't believe we were even discussing this.

Megaera sneered. "What do you care? You've got the darkness. Don't be greedy and take the light as well."

I visibly pulled back, feeling attacked. "I don't have the darkness. What does that even mean?"

Hades took that moment to enter the training room, dressed impeccably in his black and purple suit. My cheeks instantly turned red and all three of the Furies smirked.

"You know what it means," Tisiphone murmured under her breath.

"How goes the training?" he asked, looking at the

three sisters.

"We haven't yet started," Allecto said. "We were just showing young Melany here our spoils of battle."

"Ah yes, Charon informed me that we would be having chimera soup for dinner. It's been a long while since we've enjoyed such a delicacy."

All three of the Furies nodded and smacked their black lips together.

My stomach churned at the thought of eating anything remotely related to that dreadful monster.

"I have business to discuss with your trainee," he said to them.

One by one they left us alone, but both Tisiphone and Megaera gave me snide sideways glances before flying away.

Finally, Hades looked at me. But nothing in his face or eyes gave any indication that he was thinking or had thought about our coupling last night. "I trust you slept well."

"Yup. I sure did." If he wasn't going to address it, then I wouldn't either. What a jerk!

"A courier arrived earlier with a message from the academy."

I perked up at that.

"It seems Zeus plans on hosting a grand ceremony to celebrate the cadets who fought back the fire. I think there might even be medals." He sneered. "Tacky, but that's my brother for you. Of course, we are invited to the event, since we really did most of the work."

My eyes narrowed at him. "We? Don't you mean,

me? I was the one who put out most of the fire and fought the chimera."

"If I recall, you used my hound and my Furies along with my weapons to make that fight."

I couldn't believe we were having this conversation. It was ridiculous.

I shook my head and smirked. "You're a jerk." Then I stomped out of the training room.

It may have been childish, but I was feeling a bit raw. Last night was an important moment, I thought, between us. But he was acting like nothing had happened, that it was just another ordinary day in hell.

I didn't want to go back to my room and look at my bed and be reminded of our incredible sex session, so I went to the library. When I stepped inside the room, Hades was already there waiting for me. He must've zipped through the shadows, anticipating my destination.

"What's the problem?" he asked.

Pressing my lips together, I lifted my chin and met his gaze defiantly. "Nothing. Everything is just perfectly peachy."

He sighed and rubbed a hand over his face. "Are you angry I didn't stay and sleep in your bed?"

"No." Was I angry about that? Maybe. I didn't want to be some random hook-up.

"I'm no good at this…stuff." He shuffled from one foot to the other. It was the first time I'd ever seen him flustered. "I'm still your patron. We still must maintain a professional relationship, especially in front of others who work for me. You do understand that, right?"

I dropped my gaze, feeling foolish. I hated the emotions surging through me. I never thought I would be one of those girls, who pined away for any kind of attention or affection from the guy who they found attractive.

Hades was so not just some guy. We didn't just hook up. Our relationship went beyond anything normal or usual. This wasn't high school or college. This was Demigods' Academy, and I was being trained to defend the world from monsters. I needed to get over my needy bullshit.

After a moment, I nodded. "I get it. I'm sorry for being—,"

His fingers caressed my chin, and he lifted my head to look me in the eye. "No, don't apologize. We are in a precarious situation, which I fear neither of us knows how to maneuver."

I gave him a small smile, and his hand dropped away from my face. I wanted to reach up and cover his lips with my own, but I knew it wasn't the right time or place for that to happen. Instead, I turned away and asked about the invitation we got from the academy.

"Tell me more about this award ceremony or what-ever it is."

"It's to be a week from now, but for us that means in two days."

"What do you make of it?" I looked at him again.

He looked at me for a long moment. I sensed there

was something he wanted to tell me, but he turned away and walked to the table along the wall and poured water into two glasses.

"I'm not sure. On the surface it seems like a way to congratulate those who fought the fire, but knowing Zeus it will be something else altogether. A way to make him look good, I imagine. He is a glutton for the spotlight." He handed me the glass of water.

I drank it even though I wasn't thirsty. "Why do you dislike each other so much? What happened between you?"

He chuckled. "Oh, it's a long and involved story. Let's just say that Zeus and I have a very contentious relationship. We have different ideas about what it means to be a God."

I wanted to ask him if it was about Persephone and what exactly happened to her, but I knew he'd get angry if I did. I set the empty water glass on the table.

"I should get back to training." I moved toward the door.

"Let's play hooky today."

I turned and made a comical face. "Really?"

"Yeah. If you could do anything, anything at all, what would you want to do today?"

"Are you being serious right now?"

His eyebrow went way up. "I'm always serious."

"Okay. I really miss carnival season."

His eyebrow stayed up as he stared at me.

"You know, Ferris wheels, cotton candy, stupid games to win big stupid stuffed animals. Pecunia always had a great spring carnival. I would go with Callie and her friends, even though they didn't like me. I'd walk down the midway and eat all the different foods until I was almost sick. Then, I would go on the Ferris wheel when it turned dark and look out over the whole town."

"All right." He set his water glass down then offered me his hand. "Take my hand."

I frowned. "What? Why?"

"Just trust me."

Did I trust him? I looked into his dark eyes, then reached out and joined my hand with his. He linked his fingers with mine and smiled. "Hang on. This is going to be a wild ride."

Together we stepped into the shadows. My heart dropped into my stomach as we whooshed though the darkness. It was like the one time I went skiing in the Alps with the Demos family and I lost control and almost went over a jump. I concentrated on the feel of Hades's hand to keep me grounded.

A couple of minutes later, we stepped out into the showroom of what appeared to be a small costume shop. A short plump man scurried out from the back room. He bowed his head.

"Lord Hades, a pleasure to see you again so soon," the man said in a heavily accented voice.

"Francois, please outfit the lady in proper attire for the season."

The man rushed toward me and took my hand. "I am thinking something dark and fierce."

Hades smiled. "Naturally."

"What's going on?"

"Just go with him. You'll thank me later."

I let Francois lead me into a dressing room. A half hour later I walked out in a short yet puffy dark blue and black dress with fishnet stockings and knee-high black boots. On my head was a large hat also dark blue and black with feathers and lace. I looked like a cross between Marie Antoinette and Pink.

Hades waited for me in the showroom. He was dressed stylishly in a dark blue suit jacket with a long tail and high collar, his shirt was frilly, his pants tight, his boots pointy toed and polished to a shine. His dark hair was slicked back, and he wore a lacy black half mask on his spectacular face. It made his cheekbones pop. He nearly stole my breath when I looked at him.

But it was his grin when he saw me that made my belly clench.

"You look extraordinary."

I blushed. "Thank you."

"Turn around."

I did as he asked, and he came up behind me and gently affixed a lace mask like his over my face. When I turned around, his gaze lit up. "Perfect."

"What is all this?" I asked, still completely confused.

He offered me his hand again. Francois opened the door, and Hades led me outside and into a massive buoyant crowd of people in colorful costumes and masks. Lively music filled the square.

"I can't promise you there's cotton candy, but there is a Ferris wheel." He gripped my upper arms and turned me to the right where I spied the tallest Ferris wheel I'd ever seen over the tops of the stone buildings.

"Where are we?"

"Nice."

"France?"

He nodded and looked out over the huge colorful crowd. "Yes, it was the only carnival I could think of to take you to." He tugged on my hand. "C'mon, let's see if they have some cotton candy."

CHAPTER SIX

MELANY

*H*ades led me through the square. We stepped on the mass of colorful flowers that were strewn over the ground by people on the parade floats. It was part of the Battle of the Flowers, which Hades explained happened every year at the carnival. Regardless, it was like walking on rainbows and I laughed.

In the square, there were several musicians and dancers and street artists to entertain the crowds. It was all animated and vibrant and loud, and I loved it. I stopped to watch an artist, wearing a gas mask and gloves, use spray paint and various metal objects to paint the most spectacular picture of the moon and stars reflected in a quiet pool of water. It was the most beautiful thing I'd ever seen. When he was done, everyone clapped. Hades stepped up and handed him a wad of money to buy the painting for me. I didn't know how much money it had been, but the guy's eyes widened and he kept thanking Hades and me while bowing his head.

When Hades gave me the painting, I was stunned. "You can put it up on the wall in your room. It would match the décor," he said with a twinkle of humor in his eyes.

While we continued strolling around, I had to keep readjusting my grip on the painting. Although I loved it, it was awkward to hold. "Is there somewhere I can drop this off and pick it up later?"

"I have something better." He grabbed my hand and pulled me into a narrow alleyway between two old stone buildings. He found a dim corner and leaned into the shadows and shouted. "Charon!"

No more than thirty seconds later, the skeletal butler hovered in the shadows. "Yes, my Lord?"

He handed the painting to Charon. "Take this to Melany's room."

Skeletal hands clutched the paper. "Right away, my Lord."

"But don't you dare hang it on the wall without her permission, like you did with that portrait Pablo painted of me a hundred years ago. You have no sense for decorating."

Charon nodded, then vanished inside the darkness.

I laughed, which seemed to please Hades. He grabbed my hand again and led me out of the alley and back into the frivolity. We came across several food stands. There was no cotton candy unfortunately, but Hades bought me something even better—a ganses. It was a deep-fried pastry, much like a croissant, served warm with a light sprinkling of powdered sugar. It melted in my mouth. It was the most delicious thing I'd ever tasted. After finishing one, I demanded another. He obliged me with a chuckle.

For the rest of the day and well into the evening, Hades indulged my every wish. We ate and drank, listened to music, and watched the different street artists including a magician and juggler. I even danced with a man with a huge papier-mache head. I felt lighter and freer than I'd ever been in my life, which was so surprising considering my company. Who would have thought I would have the most delightful day of fun and frivolity with the God of darkness? It seemed impossible, but it was happening.

And to top it all off, when the sun set and the colorful lights of the carnival glowed over the old city and sparkled on the clear blue water of the Mediter-ranean, Hades took me on the Ferris wheel.

My stomach did a few flip flops as the wheel spun us up to the very top and stopped. I could see every-thing. The dancing lights of blue and red and green, the vibrant costumes of all the revelers as they converged into the square and started to dance to the lively music coming from the sound stage constructed in the market. I looked out over the sea; several boats and yachts had strings of white lights twinkling over their bows and masts.

I looked over at Hades as his gaze swept the scenery. The look on his face was as soft as I'd ever seen it. "Thank you for this."

His gaze swiveled onto me and he smiled. "You're most welcome."

My belly clenched, and my heart skipped a few beats. *Shit.* I was falling in love with him.

"We should probably return home soon," he said. "We will both need some sleep before the ceremony at the academy tomorrow. We'll both need to be in fine form."

I was about to ask him why we needed to be in fine form when a sudden drop in temperature sent a shiver over my body. Our passenger car started to rock back and forth as wind whipped around us.

Over the water, I could see thick dark storm clouds rolling in like an avalanche would move snow down a mountain. The unusual sight made the little hairs on the back of my neck rise. Down below, I saw crowds of people stopping to stare at the incoming storm.

"That doesn't look normal," I said.

Hades's expression matched what I felt inside. "No, it doesn't. We need to get out of this pod." He stood to inspect the door. "There aren't enough shadows in here, so we'll have to go out the old-fashioned way." He pressed his hand against the metal and pushed. The lock didn't stand a chance and the door swung open. Violent wind instantly whipped inside and yanked at my hat, pulling it off and blowing it outside. I watched as it swirled around then dropped to the ground.

Hades positioned himself at the opening of the pod. His wings broke through the back of his suit jacket but didn't fully unfurl. There wouldn't have been enough room inside if they had. "Come behind me and wrap your arms around my waist."

"I have wings. You don't need to carry me." I urged them out just a little.

"I know, but it will be easier for you to unfold them once we are in the air."

Seeing the logic, I wrapped my arms around him from behind. Just as he took a step out, the wheel started to move knocking us both into the side of the pod. Obviously, the attendants understood the need to get the people off the ride as soon as possible. The storm was nearly here. The wind had picked up, and it was making waves on the water. I could hear people shouting on the boats, trying to get to dock before it was too late.

Hades held onto the metal spoke, trying to get balanced again. I nearly slipped down his body and fell. Lightning quick, he snatched my arm and held me up until I could unfurl my wings.

I did, which proved to be a little harder in the violent wind, but eventually I was able to let go of him and get airborne. Hades pushed away from the wheel and flew after me. I struggled to fly straight and kept getting blown sideways. I collided into Hades, and he had to put an arm around me to help me stay in the air.

As we flew down beyond the square and to the shore of the harbor, people shouted and pointed up at us. I imagined we looked like harbingers of death, both wearing black with our large black wings, to the regular people below, compounded by the turbulent storm blowing in. In my mind, we looked wicked and fierce as hell.

We landed on the boardwalk overlooking the water, as waves crashed over and soaked our feet. I could see the waves were getting higher and more powerful with each passing second. But where was the rain? Surely the black clouds should've let loose already. And where were the lightning and thunder? I expected the sky to be lit up by white bolts zigzagging across the black backdrop.

I glanced at Hades. He stared out over the water, his brow deeply furrowed. "This isn't a storm, is it?"

"No. It's something else entirely."

A booming sound arose from the water. It wasn't the crack of lightning but the whoosh of something large emerging from the depths of the sea. A wave, twenty feet high, surged toward the shore, but inside that wave I swore I saw a monstrous form, just as high, with horns and scales chopping at the water.

"What is that?" I had to speak up over the roar of the approaching wave.

"Not what, who." Hades grabbed my hand, and we shot up into the air as the water crashed down on the boardwalk, smashing the wooden planks. Horrified I saw several people swallowed up by the wave and tossed out to sea.

"We have to save them."

Hades nodded, and together we swooped toward the water. I spotted an elderly man thrashing about, his head going under with every roll of a wave. I dove for him, not caring about getting wet, grabbed him around the waist and pulled him out of the water. He screamed as I flew him over to the safety of land and dropped him there. A few people who had witnessed what I'd done ran over to the man and helped him. Next to him, Hades set down a girl, no older than six. The old man opened his arms to her, and I realized that she was his granddaughter.

Hades hovered above them. "Go! It isn't safe here. Get as far inland as you can. Tell others!"

They heeded his warning and ran for the square, shouting at other people to run and get away from the harbor.

He turned back to the turbulent water. I hovered next to him. "Is it a Titan?"

"Yes. It's Oceanus. He's been locked away in Tartarus for over a thousand years. There's no way out of that prison."

"He's obviously been released, just like before, with the earthquake in Pecunia," I said. Then something occurred to me. "Who knew we were here?"

"I told no one. I didn't even know we were coming here until we left."

"I don't believe in coincidences. Do you?" I asked.

"No, I don't."

"What are we going to do?"

"Find out why Oceanus is here."

Hades flew out over the water, I joined him. More waves crashed onto the harbor, breaking it apart and surging out into the town square. Thankfully, the crowd had dispersed, heeding Hades's warning, but a few stragglers remained, taking cell phone videos.

"We're going to need weapons," I said. "How do we fight a water entity?"

"With the darkness." He slapped his hands together and rubbed them. When he pulled them apart again, a black form forged between them. Long, narrow, eventually I could make out a shape. He'd constructed a sword from shadow and night.

He tossed it to me. I caught it surprised how substantial it was. I'd expected it to be as light as air, not heavy like steel. I sliced the air in front of me with it, testing its quality. It seemed to be as expertly crafted as a sword from Hephaistos.

"How is this going to damage a creature made of water?"

"Shadow is devoid of light. The dark is without warmth. Darkness is cold and unyielding. It will freeze the water even as it cuts through it." After making himself a sword, Hades dove toward another thirty-foot wave. But this wave moved around and flailed a giant serpent-like tail into the air.

I followed Hades into battle.

As we neared the Titan, Oceanus opened his

muzzle, revealing rows of razor-sharp teeth, and roared. The closer I got the more of the creature I could see. Oceanus looked like a dragon standing upright with four curved horns protruding from his heavily scaled head. His barrel chest also looked armored with thick dark scales. The creature appeared to be impenetrable. I didn't know how our shadow swords were going to do anything but piss him off.

When Hades swooped toward him from the side, he turned and swiped a very large, very muscular arm at the God. Claws as long as my arm came close to taking Hades's head clean off. Instead, Hades swung his sword, and the blade hit the Titan's bicep. I saw the tip freeze the creature's flesh. He roared again, this time in pain.

Buoyed by what I'd seen, I flew at the beast from the opposite side, hoping Hades was distracting him enough. I drew in close and swung my sword at his head, aiming for one of the horns. My blade struck, reverberated up my arms, but my blow broke his horn in half. It cracked apart like ice.

He swung his head toward me and roared again. The blast of his breath blew me backward. I dipped down toward the water, and I spied a bit of gold around the Titan's neck. I knew what it was instantly.

I flew over to Hades, close enough for him to hear me over the rush of water and roar of the Titan. "He has a golden rope around his neck. He's being controlled."

He nodded. "Then we have to cut it off. It's the only way to stop him."

"You distract him and I'll go—,"

"No. It's too dangerous."

"He won't be expecting me, I'm smaller than you are. And honestly I'm quicker." I smirked.

He shook his head, but I could see that he knew my plan made sense. "Come at him from under his head. He won't be able to see you. He'll be glaring at me."

Before I could fly off, he snatched my hand. His gaze searched my face, as if he was trying to memorize what I looked like. I thought he was going to say something, but he let go of my hand and swooped toward Oceanus.

As Hades hovered near the Titan's face, I could see his lips moving. He was talking to him, but I couldn't hear what he was saying. The water beast was distracted, and I needed to make my move. I dove down toward the water. Right before I was swept up in the waves that the Titan made with his huge body, I arched upward. I flew so close to him that I could see the intricate patterns on the scales that surrounded his ribs. I could see the rise and fall of his chest as he breathed.

I raised my sword just as Oceanus swiped at Hades again. A wave as high the beast himself surged toward Hades. The water was going to swallow him up. There was nothing I could do about it. I had to cut the rope. It was the only way.

When I was right under his muzzle, I swung my

sword at the rope around his neck. The blade hit but didn't cut the golden threads. One blow wasn't enough. I reached for the rope with my left hand as I hacked and slashed at it. The Titan shook his head trying to dislodge me, but I hung on with all I had. Positioning myself against the rigid scales just under his chin, digging my feet into his flesh, I kept swinging my sword. I was like a mad woman as I hacked over and over again. Until finally, the threads gave way.

I fell into the surging water, but at least I had the rope clutched in my hand. I'd stopped the Titan and I had the proof of Aphrodite's treachery.

CHAPTER SEVEN

MELANY

The second I hit the water I got sucked under in a tide pool caused by the erratic movements of the Titan. Flailing my arms, I kicked hard to push myself upward, but I got sucked back down again. I tried to calm my mind so I wouldn't panic. Luckily, I could hold my breath for a long time.

I kicked my legs again to propel myself away from the beast's thick powerful legs, but he moved and I smacked my head right into him. The blow obscured my vision in the murky water, and I couldn't see where I was going. I reached out my hand. My fingers brushed against hard scales, and I brought my feet up and tried to kick away from him again.

I didn't get very far before I was scooped up by a large clawed hand. I thought about fighting against it but realized when I came sputtering out of the water that Oceanus was saving me. He held me up toward Hades who hovered near the Titan's head.

"Thank you, my friend," Hades said.

"Your human is plucky." Oceanus's voice boomed all around me. It was like a foghorn, deep and air rattling.

"Yes, she is." I was about to argue that I wasn't *his* human, but Hades turned away from me and put his attention on the giant water dragon. "Do you remember how you got here, Oceanus?"

He shook his big head. "No."

"Do you know who put this rope around your neck?"

I held up the golden tie for him to see.

His dragon eyes narrowed as he studied the rope. "No, but it must've been one of you, as you are the only beings with the keys to Tartarus."

"Well, it wasn't me," Hades said.

"I know. You are not like your brothers who only care about power." Oceanus's gaze fixed on the shore and the destroyed harbor. "Did I kill anyone?"

Hades shook his head. "No. But it was lucky that we were here."

He nodded. "Yes. Lucky." His other hand went up to his head and I realized he was feeling for any damage we'd caused him.

"I'm sorry about your horn," I yelled up at him.

His dark eyes fixed on me, and I realized he could squish me into goo if he wanted. "It will grow back."

"I fear that there will be more Titans released soon. Someone is trying to start a war," Hades said.

"I cannot return to Tartarus to warn my brethren, but I will find a place to hide and wait. If you need my assistance when the time comes, you only need to call me back."

Hades flew over to me and dropped onto the Titan's hand. "Thank you. I wish you well." He grabbed my hand and pulled me up into the air. The feathers on my wings were still damp, so I appreciated Hades's help to stay airborne.

The moment we were away, Oceanus sunk back down into the water. From up above, I could see him swimming down into the depths of the sea. When he was gone, the black clouds overhead dissipated to reveal the bright moon and a twinkling carpet of stars.

Hades flew us back to shore. The second my feet touched down, I was looking for the shadows to take us to the academy. "We need to take this to Zeus. He'll have to believe me now about Aphrodite's scheme."

"No."

I frowned. "What do you mean no? We have to tell him and the others about this."

"We will, but not now. We need to wait for the right moment, the most opportune moment." He took my arm and directed me toward a dark grouping of shadows. We stepped into the darkness, and within seconds we emerged back in the hall.

"I don't understand." I held up the thick golden rope. "We have proof."

"That could belong to anyone, Melany."

"But it's made from Aphrodite's clothes—,"

"Do you know how many ropes and belts and chains she's made for others over the past thousand years? Hundreds. She made me a rope once over four hundred years ago. It proves nothing except that Oceanus was compelled to destroy."

My shoulders sagged. I thought this was undeniable proof, but now I realized why Zeus hadn't done anything before when I showed him the rope that I found in Pecunia next to the destroyed Demos's estate. I felt like an idiot. Had I been wrong about Aphrodite and Ares all along? Had I attacked her for no reasons except for my uncontrolled fury toward her?

Hades took the rope from me. "Let me hold onto this until it's time to use it."

For a moment, I considered snatching it back from him and jumping into a shadow to go to the academy on my own. But I resisted.

"The best way to snare a fox is to lure it out into the open, then whack," he slapped his hands together, and I flinched, "pull the rope tight around its throat to snap its neck."

"I take it Aphrodite is the fox in this scenario?"

"Yes, and others."

I regarded him curiously. "I didn't realize that you were close with the Titans. I was surprised by your conversation with Oceanus."

"The Titans are not the monstrous violent beings

that you've been taught. History is always written by those in power, and it's not always the actual truth."

"So, what is the truth, then?"

Instead of answering, he reached out and feathered his fingertips down my cheek, then tucked some stringy strands of my blue hair behind my ear. "You should shower and change. We need to be at the academy in a few hours."

My heart fluttered from his light touch. I had to stop myself from breaching the distance between us, grabbing him by the shirt front and kissing him. My entire body thrummed with desire.

Then he dropped his hand and walked away. He went into the library and closed the door. I went to my room and did as he suggested. My clothes were still damp, and I smelled like brine and seaweed. As I stood under the hot spray of the shower, I half-expected Hades to walk into the bathroom and join me. I wanted him to. Even now, even though I knew he was keeping things from me, I ached for him.

Since it was going to be some kind of award cere-mony according to the courier who sent the message to Hades, I opted for an elegant dress, dark purple with spaghetti straps and a slit up the side. Charon helped me with my hair. Over the months, I'd learned that the scary butler was an expert stylist. He did a Dutch braid bun that I couldn't even begin to understand. I did some heavy makeup, a smoky eye and dark lip. When I looked in the mirror, I thought "Damn! I'm smoking hot!"

That was confirmed when I walked out into the hall where Hades waited for me. His eyebrows lifted, and his lips twitched upward into a long lazy grin that sent shivers down my back. He licked his lips while his gaze lingered on the leg teased by the slit in the dress, then up to the plunging V neck that clung seductively to my breasts.

"You…" He licked his lips again, and I reveled in the fact that I'd made him speechless. "You look delectable."

I couldn't stop the smile or the color in my cheeks. His choice of words sent a very vivid image of sex in my mind. "You do, too."

And he did. The man could wear the shit out of a suit. It fit in a way that was elegant but also sexy. There was no mistaking the lean powerful body under the black fabric of his pants and shirt. This time he opted for a dark blue jacket. It gleamed in the firelight when he stepped closer to me.

I lifted my head toward him, hoping he would kiss me. He stopped a foot away from me, raking his gaze over me again. My lips parted with a sigh of desire. Kiss me! I wanted to scream at him. He was teasing me. Just being near him, like this, was torture. And he knew it.

Finally, blissfully, he dipped his head down. His lips brushed against mine. It was just a soft caress, but it stole my breath, and I felt faint afterward. When he pulled back, he traced his finger over my cheek again. Then he took a step away and offered me his arm.

"Shall we? We're just the right amount of late to make a memorable appearance."

Chuckling, I took his arm, and we stepped into the shadows.

When we came out of the darkness and appeared in the great hall, there was a collective gasp from those in attendance. A surge of arrogance filled me, and I lifted my head and met the gazes of my peers and the other Gods gaping at us.

"Are we late?" Hades's playful grin was full of spite.

Zeus greeted us with his own poisonous smile. "Of course not. We've not even started the festivities yet." His eyes went to me. "Melany, you look stunning. Your friends have been anxiously awaiting your arrival." He waved his hand toward Jasmine, Georgina, Ren, and Mia who were grouped together gaping at me. "Why don't you join them while Hades joins the professors."

Hades took my hand, kissed the back, then gave me a little bow. I knew he did it to get a reaction. And he most definitely got one. I saw many shocked faces and I heard someone in the crowd whisper the word, "Slut." I scanned the crowd, certain it was Revana who spoke, but was surprised to see it was someone I didn't know.

Hades walked away with Zeus, while I joined my friends. Or at least, I hoped they were still friends. The way Jasmine looked at me put that in question.

Georgina approached me first, grabbing my hands, as if months hadn't passed and we were still roommates trying to survive our first year at the academy. "You look incredible."

"Thank you, Gina. So, do you." And she did. The green dress she wore, short but flirty, accentuated the muscles she'd developed over the past term. Her earth powers emanated from her and her skin seemed to glow with vitality.

Jasmine's gaze wasn't as complimentary. "You look like him."

I knew the "him" she meant. Hades.

The well-aimed barb hurt, but I tried to keep it from my face.

"Thank you," I said with a sardonic arch to my eyebrow. I looked past her, letting her know I was pissed at her. "Where's Lucian? Is he out of the infirmary?"

"Blue?"

I turned toward his voice. He crossed the room toward me, a smile on his face. He looked amazing in a royal blue tunic and white pants. His blond hair was slicked back from his face. Despite his trip into death, there was a radiance that shone through his eyes.

He looked me up and down. "You look like a Goddess."

It was the perfect thing to say.

I went to him and hugged him close, inhaling his warmth. "I'm so happy to see you."

"Me too." He nuzzled his face into the side of my neck. "I didn't think I'd see you here."

I pulled back. "Why not? It's supposed to be a cele-bration, isn't it? You didn't think I'd be invited?"

He shook his head. "It isn't that."

His gaze drifted across the room and settled on

Hades who was talking to Dionysus. He turned slightly, his eyes meeting Lucian's and he tipped his head. Something passed between them. I didn't know what it was, but I could tell Lucian was angry about it.

"What is that all about?" I demanded. "What is going on between the two of you?"

Before he could answer though, Zeus lifted his hand to quiet the soft violin music that had been playing, then he began to talk.

CHAPTER EIGHT

MELANY

"*W*elcome all." Zeus's voice boomed throughout the room. "Tonight, we celebrate the achievements of this academy and honor those who have brought great glory and recognition to our institution."

That brought a round of applause throughout the room.

"The fire at Victory National Park was handled quickly and efficiently by our cadets with very few casualties. Our friends in the country's government were very thankful for our assistance and assured us that this was just one step closer to an integration of our warriors into their system."

I frowned. I didn't know how Zeus could consider it a success when there had been loss of lives. Several firefighters had died from the chimera's attack. Lucian had died, technically. I couldn't keep silent.

"What about the chimera?" I said loudly, stepping away from my friends and toward the Gods who stood up on the dais at the front of the room. "It was responsible for several human casualties."

I could hear Hades sigh. He wasn't subtle about it. I also was keenly aware that Aphrodite was shooting daggers from her eyes my way.

A wave of animated murmurs surrounded me.

"The chimera's appearance was unexpected," Zeus said. "But was handled with the utmost delicacy and candor by those on the frontlines. We have you to thank, Melany, do we not? For the quick dispatchment and disposal of the creature." He smiled at me as if I was supposed to be delighted by his praise.

I took another step forward, intending to lambaste him for his complacency and to demand that an investigation be mounted to find out who released the beast into the park.

Hades also stepped forward. "The chimera's appearance was indeed a surprise, and I know I can speak for the rest of the professors that we will find out how the creature arrived in the forest and why." His gaze swept over the Gods in attendance, lingering a little longer on Aphrodite and Ares I was happy to see. "It will not go unanswered, I assure you."

Zeus nodded. "Quite right."

I was about to speak again, but Hades glared at me, telling me to stop before I put my foot into my mouth again. I did but only because Lucian moved in beside me. I didn't want to drag him down into what I was sure was going to be my downfall.

But I couldn't hold my tongue. "I expect that the families of those fallen firefighters will be fully compensated for their loss. A year's favor from all the Gods wouldn't be too much to ask."

There were gasps from my fellow cadets at the gall I had to demand such things from the Gods. I knew I was pushing my luck, but I was tired of the games they were playing. They were all culpable, even Hades. It was obvious that he was playing his own game and not letting me in on the stakes or rules.

Lucian set his hand on my arm and whispered, "What are you doing?"

Aphrodite smirked. "Your request comes with the assumption that we had something to do with the chimera."

I could hear Hades's voice in my head. "Don't you dare do it."

"The chimera is a creature of your world. It's your responsibility, isn't it?" More gasps from my peers and a few stunned faces of the demigods in attendance. Heracles looked like he wanted to hide in a cave on my behalf. "As are the Titans who you locked away in Tartarus. If one were to escape, that would be your responsibility too, wouldn't it? I mean, you're the only ones with the key."

I saw Dionysus shake his head and say, "Oh, shit."

Demeter covered her face with her hand. I could just imagine the words she mumbled under her breath.

The other Gods all looked like they wanted to kill me, even Hephaistos. Before any of them could react though, Hades flew off the dais and scooped me up and flew us out of the room. He set me down just outside the looming doors.

"What are you trying to do?" he demanded. His eyes flashed with his inner fire.

"More than what you're doing. I'm rattling cages to see what falls out."

"An axe to your head is what is going to fall out if you're not careful." He scrubbed at his chin. "Zeus is not a patient man. He'll only put up with so much insubordination."

"Is that what happened between you two? You lipped him off one too many times?"

His gaze raked me over the coals. "You need to stop talking about things you know nothing about. You're being a stupid girl here. You need to learn when to keep your mouth shut."

His tone made me shake. I bit down on my bottom lip to keep from either screaming or crying; I wasn't sure which I wanted to do more. I hated that he talked to me like I was some child, one of his students that he needed to be chastised for doing something wrong.

I thought I was more to him than that.

I kept his gaze, refusing to give him the satisfaction of my compliance. He stared back at me, breathing hard out his nose. I fully expected to see smoke curling out of his nostrils.

Gods, I wanted to kiss him right there and then. What would he do, if I did? Grab me? Slam me up against the wall? Kiss me until I couldn't breathe? Rip off my panties and thrust himself inside me until I screamed in ecstasy?

Before I could respond to him, we were interrupted. Lucian came to my side.

"Is there a problem, here?"

Hades gaze briefly flitted over to Lucian, then he sniffed and shook his head. "Maybe you can put some sense into her head. I'm going to go back and try to save her life. Again." Without looking at me, he marched back into the great hall to talk to Zeus.

After he was gone, Lucian touched my shoulder and he noticed that I was shaking. "Are you okay, Blue? What did that asshole do to you?"

I let go of a shaky breath. "Nothing."

"I don't believe you." He cupped my face in his hand. "You can talk to me, Blue. You can tell me anything."

But I can't, Lucian. Don't you see? I was sure he wouldn't want to know how much I wanted Hades, how I was falling for him, even as I wanted Lucian, right now. He wouldn't be able to understand how I could feel so much, so intensely for them both.

"Can I have a hug?" I finally said.

"Always." He gathered me into his arms, and it was like embracing the sun. Warmth surged over me, through me. My body stopped shivering. I no longer felt like I wanted to cry. Lucian was calm and comfort for me, the exact opposite of what Hades represented. Light to his dark.

And I hated myself for it, but I wanted, no needed, both in my life.

I lifted my chin and found his mouth. Reaching up, I sunk my hands into his soft golden waves and kissed him hard. I knew I'd taken him by surprise, so he was unsure at first, but it didn't take long for him to grip me around the waist and kiss me back. Just as hard, just as eager, just as lost as I was, searching for something to make sense.

And Lucian made sense. I knew he did. But it still didn't stop me from wanting Hades to return from the great hall to wrap me up in darkness and spirit me away down to the Underworld, back to his bed.

How despicable would I be if I enticed Lucian to make love to me right here, right now, to help me purge the darkness from my mind, body, and soul?

I decided not to test the limits of my immorality and pulled back to nestle my head against his chest and find solace in the strong vibrant beat of his heart. I sighed into him, wrapping my arms even tighter around his waist.

He ran a hand over my hair. "I'm worried about you."

"I know and I appreciate it."

"I can see his influence on you."

"And I can see Zeus's on you." I raised my head to

look him in the eyes. "And Ares's on Jasmine, and Demeter's on Gina. It's inevitable, isn't it?" I took a step away. "I mean we have their blood running through our veins." I rubbed a hand over my wrist. "It's what makes us special."

"You were special even before Hades came into the picture." He reached for my hand. "He is not what makes you special at all."

I linked my fingers with his. Gods, he was sweet. I didn't deserve him. Here I was making of mess of everything, and Lucian just wanted to make everything right again. I knew I said Zeus had influence over him, but the truth was Lucian was superior and more just than Zeus could ever hope to be. He was the best of us all.

"Why are you so good to me? I've been such a bitch lately."

His grin was quick, and he pulled me closer. He dipped his head and brushed his lips against mine. "Because I know its not your fault." Another light dusting of his lips making my belly clench. "And because I love you."

My heart swelled at his words. I stared him in the eyes, searching for a response in them. But I knew the truth, deep down inside. "I love you, too."

He kissed me again, a bit more playfully, as his hand snuck down to caress my backside. "We could go find a dark alcove and finish what we started all those months ago. Forget the ceremony." His lips trailed down to my neck and nibbled at my skin. "This dress of yours is giving me all kinds of interesting thoughts."

I was tempted. It would be easy to just sneak away down the hall, thumb our noses to duty and obligation, and just give into each other. But that wasn't who Lucian was. And I supposed that wasn't how I was either. We'd both worked hard to be in the academy, to find out respective places in the pantheon of eventual demigods. Lucian had literally died fighting that fire to save the park and the town nearby from being destroyed. He deserved to be recognized for that. I wouldn't get in the way of that, no matter how good it would feel to have his body entwined with mine.

Zeus's booming voice coming out of the great hall announcing the cadets who had risked their lives battling the inferno and the chimera kind of made that decision for us.

I pulled back from him, gave him a smile, and linked my arm around his. "Let's go get our medal, or whatever they're presenting us with, then we can have our way with each other."

Lucian laughed. "Sounds like a plan."

Together, arm in arm, we walked back into the great hall to get what we deserved. A shiver rushed down my spine as I suspected my reward wasn't going to be what I expected.

CHAPTER NINE

MELANY

I was fully aware of the way Hades glared at us when Lucian and I walked into the hall together, our arms around each other. I hated that I got pleasure out of his obvious jealousy. I glanced at Lucian and saw that he was grinding his teeth as he glared in return.

We joined Jasmine, Mia, and Georgina who were standing to the right of the dais waiting for their names to be called. Ren, Marek, Quinn, and Su had already been called up and were now standing on the stage as Hera and Aphrodite did the honors of draping gold medals hanging on silk ribbons over their heads.

Jasmine shook her head as we approached. "You're unbelievable," she said to me.

"What's your problem?" Lucian had to restrain me

from getting in her face. I had sensed this confrontation was some time coming. "If you have something to say to me, say it."

For the past few months Jasmine had been looking at me differently. I could feel our friendship drifting apart. I couldn't deny I was partly responsible for that, but she'd been displaying animosity toward me ever since my sojourn to the Underworld where I'd been training with Hades and the Furies. It was almost like she was jealous, but I didn't know why. She had Mia, and I didn't think she wanted to be with Lucian.

"Jasmine Walker," Zeus called her up to the stage.

She turned away from me and walked up the steps to join the others. Hera draped a medal around her neck, and our peers in the crowd clapped and cheered. Georgina was called next. She got louder applause led by my hands, as Aphrodite draped her medal around her neck.

"Lucian Perro."

I gave his hand a squeeze, and then he went up the steps onto the stage. Hera placed the medal around his neck, and I cheered the loudest. I thought he should get all the medals as he had died fighting the chimera. There should be something more than a silly medal for that kind of bravery.

For a moment, I thought Zeus wasn't going to call me up as punishment for speaking my mind, but then he did.

"Melany Richmond."

I wasn't sure what kind of reaction to expect from

my peers, but it most definitely wasn't the silence that accompanied me up the steps and onto the stage. I stood next to Lucian, who gave me a reassuring smile. Unfortunately, it was Aphrodite who was to put the medal around my neck, although I imagine she would've much rather have wrapped her hands around it instead.

With a saccharine smile, Aphrodite stepped in front of me. "Congratulations," she said with all the sincerity of a narcissistic psychopath.

I bent my head forward a little so she could slip the silk ribbon over it. As she did, she leaned in close to my ear. "Beware the snakes all around you. Their venom just might be the death of you some day." When she finished, she stepped back and gently clapped her hands.

There was a smattering of applause in the room. The Gods on the stage were more enthusiastic. It was obvious my peers didn't feel all that warm toward me anymore.

"Congratulations to all our heroes," Zeus said. "You are the leaders of this academy, and I look forward to seeing where you will lead us in the future."

More applause, some cheers. I spied Revana in the crowd and her deep scowl nearly made me burst out laughing. Now, she was probably regretting not volunteering to fight the fire in Victory Park. I wanted to shout out to her, "Suck it up, buttercup!" But I refrained.

"Now we celebrate!" Zeus clapped his hands

together, and the main lights dimmed while a variety of colored lights flared to life. Loud dance music blasted from the speakers strategically placed around the hall. It sounded like Dionysus was in fine form again.

Hephaistos's little serving robots zoomed into the room, carrying trays of drinks and food to everyone's delight. My stomach rumbled. I hadn't eaten since the ganses from the carnival in Nice. Thinking about that, I looked for Hades on the stage. I didn't think it was right that we hadn't told anyone about the Titan's attack. Regardless of who released Oceanus, I still thought it was prudent that we inform Zeus of what happened so the academy could prepare for another attack. Because I had no doubt, that an even bigger threat was imminent.

I caught his gaze; he was across the dais talking to Artemis. She didn't look very happy with what he was saying. I started toward him when Lucian hooked an arm around my waist and spun me around.

"Dance with me," he whispered into my ear.

I considered rejecting his request, but something about the way Hades looked at me, pissed me off, so I draped my arms around Lucian's neck and kissed him. "Let's dance."

We stepped down from the stage and joined the others who had already made space for dancing in front of Dionysus's DJ setup. Smoke was drifting across the floor and flashing strobe lights pierced the dark. It reminded me of the first night in the academy, and that first dance with Lucian when I hadn't been sure about him.

I was sure about him now.

I molded my body to his, and we moved as one to the rhythmic beat of the music. Others danced around us, but I was oblivious to them. All I could see, all I wanted to be with was Lucian. When the music slowed a little, I draped my arms over his shoulders and pressed in close to him. One of his hands gripped my waist, the other pressed against my lower back. We swayed like that, in sync, our eyes locked on each other for what seemed like an hour. I was perfectly happy to stay just like that until my stomach got the better of me and I desperately needed some food.

"I need to eat," I said to Lucian. "I'll be right back."

He kissed me on the cheek then I set off to find a plate and pile it full of food. Unfortunately, I ran into Revana and her new minions while doing so.

She looked me up and down and sneered. "Now I guess we know why you're being treated so special."

Peyton and Klara both snickered with her.

"How does it feel to be Hades's whore?"

I flinched surprised by the true malice in her voice. I clenched my hand into a fist fully intending to use it on her when both Peyton and Klara's eyes widened and they both audibly swallowed.

"Here, I brought you something to eat. You looked ravenous." Hades slid in next to me and handed me a plate with a couple of finger sandwiches and pastries on it. His gaze swept over Revana and the others, as if they were inconsequential.

"Are you going to be teaching at the academy now?" Klara asked him eagerly. I saw the dreamy look in her eyes and wanted to scratch it out.

"Gods no." He shooed them way with his hand. "Go away. You're boring me."

I had to bite my tongue to stop from laughing, as the three of them scurried away. When they were gone, I chuckled. "That was priceless. Did you see their faces?"

"What are you doing?"

I plucked one of the sandwiches from the plate. "Eating. I'm starving."

"You shouldn't be running around here on your own."

I frowned. "Why not? This is a safe place."

He didn't answer but continued to glower at me.

"We should tell Zeus about the Titan attack," I said after eating both sandwiches.

"I will when it's the right time."

"When will that be?"

He rolled his eyes. "You ask too many questions, it's exhausting."

"Maybe I'll just go back and dance with Lucian."

"Yes, maybe you should."

My eyes narrowed at him. "Why are you acting like this?"

"Like what?"

"Like you don't give a shit about our relationship."

"Relationship?" His eyebrows shot up and he smirked. "We don't have a relationship, Melany. We've had some fun, but that's about as far as that goes. I'm your teacher and you're my student."

Stunned, I flinched back as if he'd actually slapped me across the face. Tears pricked my eyes, but I refused to let them fall in front of him. He didn't deserve them. "I can't believe you said that to me."

"I don't know why."

"You're an asshole."

He shrugged. "Yes, I've been told. You should really return to Lucian. I'm sure he's worried about where you've run off to." He looked away from me and surveyed the crowd.

I shoved the plate he gave me back at him, not caring that the cream-puff pastry smooshed onto his shirt and pants. I stormed away, found Lucian at a table near the dance floor sitting with Georgina, Ren, Diego, and Rosie. When he saw me, his eyes lit up and I wanted to cry.

Instead I grabbed him by the shirt front and smashed my lips to his. I wrapped my hand in his hair and deepened the kiss until we were both breathless. When I pulled back, I was acutely aware of several sets of eyes on us. I looked for one particular set, hoping he had seen. I found him standing with Demeter and Heracles staring. For someone who didn't give a shit, he sure seemed to be angry.

I wanted to scream.

Lucian ran his hand over my arm. "Are you all right?"

I looked at him, a forced smile on my face. "I'm fine. Where's Jasmine? I think the two of us need to have a talk." My anger was swirling, and I needed it go somewhere. Not that I wanted to lash out at Jasmine, but it was obvious we needed to hash some things out. I didn't want her to hate me.

"Last I saw her she was talking to Dionysus about music." Lucian gestured with his head. "Here she comes."

I turned to see Jasmine walking toward us, carrying two drinks. When she neared, she smiled, and I felt relief surge through me. "Hey, I'm sorry about earlier. It's none of my business what's going on between you and Hades—"

"No, don't apologize. There's nothing going on, I assure you."

She nodded then offered me a glass. "A peace offering."

I glanced inside the cup, expecting soda or juice, but I was pretty sure it was wine.

She leaned in. "It's got some kick. I thought we could party a little together. We've earned it."

"We certainly have."

We tapped our glasses then I took a big swallow. It was indeed wine and definitely had a kick. I felt it the second it hit my stomach. A heat swelled inside like a tsunami. It reminded me a bit of the whiskey Hades had given me in his library. Except the whiskey hadn't burned like this did.

I swallowed, trying to subdue the burning sensation but it just seemed to be growing. My mouth was on fire.

Lucian frowned as he looked at me. "Blue?"

I pointed to my throat. "I need some water." I could barely get the words out as my throat seemed to be constricting.

"What did you give her?" Lucian demanded of Jasmine.

"Just some wine." She was now looking at me with concern as well.

Georgina came to my side with a glass of water. She took the wine away and handed me the water. I swallowed it down. It did nothing for the blistering pain in my body. I shook my head. "Something's wrong."

I couldn't stand anymore. I sagged in Lucian's arms and he carefully laid me down on the floor. By now, a bit of a crowd had gathered, murmuring to each other.

"What's wrong with her?"

"Is she sick?"

"She doesn't look good at all."

Searing pain rippled through me and my body convulsed. I curled into a protective ball to relieve the pain, but it didn't work. The pain was all through me. It felt like my insides were melting.

"Help!" Lucian called. "Someone get Chiron!"

There was a commotion around me, then the crowd parted, and Zeus and Chiron pushed through.

Chiron crouched next to me. He put his hands on my head and chest. His cool touch was a relief to the burning on my skin. He then pried open my mouth and looked inside. He winced.

"She's been poisoned."

Lucian glared at Jasmine. "What did you give her?"

"Just some wine. I swear it."

Georgina held out the glass toward Chiron. "This is what she drank from?"

Zeus snatched it from her and whirled on Jasmine, who was starting to cry. "Where did you get the wine from?"

"Dionysus," she stammered.

Everything around me started to fade. I couldn't make out distinctive voices or faces. It all became just one loud buzzing in my ears. Pain was the only thing I knew. It ate at my body and my mind. It consumed me entirely. And I realized this was what it was like to die.

CHAPTER TEN

MELANY

I woke in a field of yellow flowers with the sun beating down on me. I sat up, shielding my face from the glare of sunlight. Blinking spots from my eyes, I wondered how long it had been since I felt the warm sun on my skin. Months? A year? It felt longer than either of those.

I stood and stretched out my arms. I heard the satisfying pop of my bones aligning. I glanced down at where I was laying and wondered how long I'd been there. By the way my muscles cramped and my bones ached, it had been a long time. Longer than a night's sleep, that was for sure.

After bending and cracking my body, I surveyed my surroundings. The field of yellow stretched out in all four directions as far as I could see. I spun around in a circle, trying to get my bearings. I couldn't be sure which way was north or south or east or west. I looked up at the sun starting to arc downward, and figured I was facing west. I'd walk that way for a lack of a better plan.

As I walked, I realized I wasn't wearing any shoes. I looked down at my bare feet, wriggling my toes in the dirt. I was sure I'd recently had high heels on. Pretty fancy shoes. I also noticed I was wearing a plain white sheath dress with short sleeves. In my mind, I pictured a purple dress with a long slit along one leg. But why would I have been wearing that kind of dress? It seemed like something way too sophisticated for someone like me.

I kept walking, running my fingertips over the petals of the wildflowers. Soon, I came to a slight rise. I crested it, and at the top I stared out over a stunning valley with more flowers of every color imaginable and a narrow stream that meandered like a snake through them. Beyond that were several high rock formations, greenery wrapping around the stone like a blanket, with waterfalls cascading down the sides. On top of the middle structure was a building that looked very much like one of the Gods' temples back home.

Home? For a minute, I wondered where home was. I couldn't quite picture it. I just had flashes of darkness and fire that seemed to contradict each other but somehow felt right together.

I continued to walk through the field of flowers. When I came to the stream, I imagined a pathway through the water, then it appeared. A dirt path cut right through the stream. It seemed impossible, but I stepped onto it just the same.

After I crossed the water, I was magically at the bottom of the highest rock formation. That was how things worked in dreams. And this most definitely had to be a dream. It had that floating sensation like one. I looked up at the rock wondering how I was going to get to the top. I thought that I could use my wings.

I looked over my shoulder at my back wondering where my wings were. I was sure that I possessed a pair. Then I thought, *Why I would have wings*. That didn't make any sense. While I was debating the merits of having wings, a path erupted from the rock, winding around and around all the way to the top.

I stepped up onto the path, thinking it was going to take me a long time to reach the top, then I watched as my foot stepped onto a white cobblestone platform. I looked up to see I'd reached the top of the rock and the white stone temple loomed ahead of me.

A shudder of fear rushed through me as I mounted the steps to the temple. I didn't know why I was afraid. This didn't seem like a place to fear. It was welcoming, a place to reflect and pray. Once I mounted all the steps, I passed between two massive stone pillars and entered the building.

Inside there were plants growing out of large painted pots that were surrounding a grand stone fountain of a siren sitting on a bed of rocks. Water gushed out of her mouth and up into the air. At first, I thought the temple was empty, but then I spotted a woman, dressed in a gauzy white toga, lounging on a sofa in the corner. As I approached her, I saw she was beautiful with long black hair and vivid blue eyes. Her full lips were painted blood red, and her eyes were coaled in gold.

She smiled when she spotted me, and there was something about her that seemed familiar to me. I'd seen her before, but I couldn't quite place where or when. Maybe I'd dreamed about her before.

"Hello," she said, her voice like a musical interlude.

"Hello."

She lifted a slim hand toward me. I took it, and she gently pulled me down to sit next to her on the sofa. "I'm happy to see you, but I don't think you're supposed to be here."

"Where is here?"

"Elysium."

The sound of the word made me giggle. "I'm dead?"

"No, you're not dead."

"I must be lost then."

"Yes, you are very lost, Melany."

I frowned. "You know my name."

"Yes, I know everything about you." She grabbed both my hands in hers and smiled at me. "I've been watching over you." I liked her smile, it made me feel comforted.

"What is your name?"

"Persephone."

I smiled and repeated her name, enjoying the way it felt on my lips.

She placed a hand on my cheek. "You must listen to me, child."

My head felt floaty and drugged. "Okay," I whispered to her.

"You are the key, which is why I sent you the shadowbox during the Demos girl's birthday, since your original one was intercepted. You will be the one to end the battle. You have control of all five elements, but they must be freely given to you."

I didn't know what she was talking about, but I liked the sound of her voice. It was so melodic and silvery. I reached up and touched her hair. "You're so pretty."

"Melany, you need to hear what I'm telling you. You need to lead them. Without you, they don't stand a chance of stopping the war."

Before I could respond, two other people entered the temple from another doorway. An older man and woman. When they spotted us, they ran over, their voices and faces animated with excitement. The woman hugged me tight.

"Oh, my darling. My sweet girl."

Confused, I pulled away from her, searching her face for something. Then I saw it. Her eyes were the same as mine. The shape of her face, the cadence of her voice. It came back to me in a distressing rush, and

I cried out.

"Mom?"

Tears streamed down her face, as she nodded. "Yes, my darling. I'm your mother."

I looked up at the man, hovering right behind her. He too had tears. "Dad?"

He crouched and wrapped his arms around me. "Oh Melany. I can't believe you're here."

Persephone stood. "She's not supposed to be here. It's not her time. And you need to let her go, she has work to do."

Then like a sledgehammer to my mind, my memories surged back into my head.

My parents' death.

Sophie adopting me.

The shadowbox.

The directions to the academy.

Meeting Lucian.

The trials.

Hades.

Dying…

Gasping, I jolted to my feet, nearly knocking my dad onto his butt. He got up with me, as did my mom. They both reached out to grab one of my hands.

I started to sob. My whole body shook with them. "I miss you so much."

My dad kissed my hand. "We miss you, my darling. You have no idea how much. We never wanted to leave you. Ever."

"Our car accident wasn't an accident." My mom

squeezed my hand. "They knew about you. They knew how powerful you'd become."

"Who's they? What are you talking about?"

Persephone pulled me away from my parents. "It's time for you to go back. You've been away from your body too long already."

I grasped at my parents' hands. "No, I want to stay here."

As Persephone led me out of the temple, my parents remained where they were. They clutched each other, both crying.

"I don't know what's going on. Who would want to kill you?"

"Look into the past, Melany," my mom said. "Look into the history of the academy. You'll find us there."

Outside the temple, Persephone continued to lead me away, toward the cliff's edge. I tried to struggle against her, to go back to the temple, back to my parents, but she was strong, and something else, something unseen, compelled me to let her pull me away.

Persephone stopped at the edge of the cliff, still holding onto my arm. "It's time for you to go back."

"I don't understand what's going on. I know my parents are dead. Am I? Are you?"

She cupped my face again with her hand. "Dead is never really dead. We will see each other again."

Then she backed me up another step and pushed me off the cliff.

"Tell Hades I never left him. I was taken against my will. Tell him Zeus…"

But I didn't hear the rest of what she said as I fell from the mountain.

***

LUCIAN

Melany's whole body convulsed on the floor. Foam bubbled out between her lips. I didn't know what to do. I held her in my arms, feeling completely useless.

"Help her!" I shouted at Chiron.

He shook his head. "I can't. She's too far gone. The poison has done too much damage."

So many faces stared down at us. Jasmine had collapsed on the ground beside us, crying uncontrollably. I could hear Georgina's quiet sobs behind me. And Ren's and the others. I looked up to see Revana staring down at me, her face unreadable.

I saw some of the Gods crowd around. Demeter looked upset. Heracles, too. The looks on the others' faces were hard to make out. Unconcerned. Upset. Annoyed. I couldn't tell. Then there was Hades. He stood apart from everyone else.

Our gazes met, and something passed between us. I could hear his voice in my head.

I'm a part of you, Lucian. Remember. My power is in you.

Frowning, I looked down at Melany as she convulsed once more then slumped against me. I swallowed down my tears, my sorrow. As I did, I felt a heat along my chest. It was reminder of what Hades had done to me.

He left a scar on my chest. A scar in the shape of his hand.

Setting Melany down flat onto the ground, I lifted my hand over her, then placed it down upon her chest. I closed my eyes and poured every ounce of power I had in me into her. I poured all my thoughts, all my love, everything that made me, into her body.

I concentrated on her healing. I pictured each organ, each piece of her, and enveloped it with a power to counteract the poison. Purification to counter the decay. I poured all my positive energy into every cell of her being.

At first, I didn't think it was making a difference, but then I felt her heartbeat. It was faint at first, then strengthened with each beat. I opened my eyes to watch her face for some sign that she was healing. Her eyelids fluttered, then she coughed. I rolled her over onto her side, and she coughed up some liquid. It was the wine she drank.

There was a collective gasp throughout the room as she opened her eyes.

Relief surged through me, and I wiped the tears from my face. I rubbed a hand over her back as she hacked up more of the poison.

"Get it out, Blue. That's good."

Chiron crouched next to us. His gaze was wild as he took in Melany and me. "What did you do?"

I shook my head. "I'm not quite sure." My guts

started to cramp up. A terrible taste erupted into my mouth. I leaned over and retched. Red wine, just like what Melany had drunk, spewed from my mouth.

"You drew the poison out of her body."

I looked up to see Hades leaning over Melany. He reached for her, and his fingers brushed against her cheek.

I jumped to my feet and got right in his face. "I wouldn't have had to save her if you'd done what I told you to do. To keep her away from the ceremony."

There was a murmur in the crowd around us. I could sense everyone staring, wondering what we were talking about.

Melany coughed some more, but she was awake and lucid now, looking at me and Hades. She frowned, and with Chiron's help she got to her feet.

"What's Lucian talking about?"

Hades didn't answer. "Now that you're feeling better, we should return to the hall."

Melany turned to me. "What's going on?"

"I told Hades that there was going to be an attempt on your life tonight. I told him not to bring you here. To keep you safely away."

Melany's eyes narrowed as she regarded Hades. "Is this true?"

"I knew Lucian would save you if something were to happen. That's why I told you to stay by his side. As usual, you didn't listen." He waved a hand toward me. "But look he saved you. With my power, mind you."

She blinked at him and made a face. "Are you actually blaming me right now?"

"Of course, I'm not blaming you. You're being overly dramatic." He reached for her arm. "We can discuss it later."

She pulled away from his grasp. "No. I'm not going back with you. I'm done being your little pet project." She wrapped her hand around the amulet around her neck and tugged. The chain broke, and she tossed at him. It hit his shoe before landing on the floor.

"Oh burn, dude," someone said from the crowd hovering around. A couple other people snickered.

Hades bent to pick up the amulet. He tucked it into his jacket pocket. "Now that the show is over, I bid everyone adieu." He waved a hand in front of him, and tendrils of darkness seemed to appear from thin air. Before he disappeared, he looked at Melany. "You are part of the darkness, Melany. You'll never be done with that. You'll never be done with me." Then he was gone.

As I cradled Melany into my side, more commotion erupted around us. Uniformed guards pushed through the crowd and grabbed a hold of Jasmine. She struggled against them, but they were strong.

"What are you doing?" she shouted.

Zeus stepped forward. "I'm sorry, but we need to know who tried to kill Melany."

Melany tried to rush toward Zeus, but she was still weak. "Jasmine wouldn't try to kill me. We're friends."

Beyond the crowd, I saw more guards escorting Dionysus out of the hall. Melany must've seen it as well because she shook her head. "No way. I won't believe it."

"One way or another, we will find out the truth." Zeus turned and walked out of the room. The other Gods following in his wake.

I saw Aphrodite and Ares whispering to each other as they walked away. And I was sure Aphrodite was smiling.

CHAPTER ELEVEN

MELANY

*a*fter Jasmine and Dionysus were taken away, naturally the party ended. Zeus instructed everyone to return to their respective clan hall. I couldn't return to mine. I refused to.

"You can stay with me," Georgina said as if reading my mind. "Demeter won't mind one bit."

I nodded my thanks.

Lucian rubbed a hand over my back again. "You should let Chiron check you out to make sure you're okay."

The aforementioned healer nodded in agreement. "I concur. Although I'm getting tired of the two of you always being in my infirmary."

"Hey, if we weren't dying all the time, you'd be bored." I gave him a small smile to ease the tension in the room, although I didn't feel like smiling. I was exhausted. My trip to Elysium tired me out. And I wanted answers.

As Lucian, Georgina, and I walked together across the academy to meet Chiron in the infirmary, I started asking questions.

"How did you know someone was going to try and kill me?"

Lucian grimaced. "When I was recovering in the infirmary, I heard someone talking about it."

"Who?"

He shrugged. "I couldn't be sure. I was in a place between awake and asleep and couldn't tell who was in the room or who was speaking. I just heard the words spoken. When I finally woke up, there were quite a few people in the room."

"Tell me who."

"Zeus, Chiron, Ares, Aphrodite, Demeter, Dionysus, and Heracles."

"It has to be Aphrodite and Ares. The others would never conspire against me." Wincing, I rubbed my forehead. I was starting to get a headache. A bad one. "They would have no reason."

"You need to sleep," Georgina said.

"I need to get Jasmine out of wherever they took her. It's not right. She was obviously set up to take the fall."

"We will." Lucian put his arm around me. "You don't have to do all of this alone."

After Chiron did a thorough examination and I

refused his offer of convalescing in the infirmary, I marched out of there hell bent on finding out where Jasmine was. But when I stormed down the hallway, I collapsed. My legs didn't work all that well. My entire body was trying to heal the damage the poison had inflicted on me.

Lucian picked me up. "You're going to go with Gina and get some sleep."

"But—"

"I will do some snooping around and find out where Jasmine is and what is going to happen to her."

I nodded when I what I really wanted to do was to slide into one of the shadows and find Zeus to demand that he release Jasmine. But I could hardly move. Dying was catching up to me. Georgina took over the holding me up duties and led me to her hall, while Lucian set off to find out about Jasmine.

We walked to the far east corner of the academy. The doors to Demeter's Hall were tall like all the other halls, but they were made of white wood instead of stone or metal with intricate patterns carved into them. I had sense if I touched them, they would pulse with the power of nature. When we neared, they opened, and Georgina helped me to hobble inside.

I was immediately struck by the beauty of the hall and the floral scent that perfumed the air. Flowers of every color sprouted from small pots, big pots, long planters, and some even seemed to be growing right out of the floor. Other flowers and vines hung down from upside down planters sweeping along the ceiling. A waterfall cascaded down one wall, filling a lagoon populated with more plants, fish, and frogs. The domed ceiling seemed to emanate sunlight. I raised my face to it and smiled; it reminded me of my dream.

I must've gasped, because Georgina chuckled. "It's amazing, isn't it?"

"It is. I think it's my favorite hall in the academy."

Georgina squeezed me around the waist. "I'm so happy you're here. I know it's under crappy circumstances, but I'm pleased just the same."

"Me too."

And it was nice to have a moment's reprieve just to relax with my friend.

She led me to her room, which was a small alcove just past the waterfall. "You take the bed. I'll sleep on the floor."

"I can't put you out like that, Gina."

She grabbed another blanket and put it on the floor. "You aren't. Besides that, out of the two of us, you died. So, you kind of win on who deserves the bed more." She opened one of her dresser drawers and took out a pair of sweatpants and a T-shirt and handed them to me. "Thought maybe you'd want to change. You can't possibly sleep in that gorgeous dress."

I hugged her close. "I've missed you."

"Me too."

After I changed, the pants were a bit short and the T-shirt a bit loose, but I was thankful for them. I sat on the bed and regarded my friend. She'd really blossomed in the past six months. She wasn't the timid girl I'd tripped over on the dorm room floor. "You look happy here."

She sat cross-legged on the blanket. "I am. Demeter has been an incredible mentor. She's taught me so much."

"That's awesome." I brought my knees up to my chest and hugged my legs.

For a moment, it felt like we were back in our dorm room, and it was the first week of being at the academy. We were both so unsure and scared of what we'd been drawn into. Now, we were on the cusp of fulfilling our destinies as soldiers in the Gods Army. Except it wasn't as simple as that. And I started to question exactly what we'd been conscripted to fight for.

I didn't think the Gods were all on the same page. There were conflicting goals. It felt like everyone had an agenda.

"I'm worried about Jasmine," I said.

"Me too. You don't think she had anything to do with poisoning you?"

"Gods no. She may have been angry at me, but I know she loves me, as I love her. Like I love you. You're my best friends." I could feel tears welling in the corner of my eyes. It was strange how many emotions I had bubbling up to the surface since being away from Hades's Hall. I hadn't realized how much that place had influenced me, how much it and Hades had changed me.

"She wasn't angry with you, just worried. You know how she gets."

I nodded. "I know."

Georgina reached under her bed and pulled out a big bag of chips. I laughed as she ripped them open, ate some, then handed it to me. "We can't have a girls' night without snacks."

I took some chips and ate them. It had been a long time since I'd just hung out with anyone. Maybe back home. Despite the animosity between Callie and me over the years, we did have a few nights of just sitting around, eating junk food and watching a movie. Callie would paint her toenails, and on a rare night she would paint mine for me.

It had been a long time since I thought about her and about Pecunia. I pushed most of it down, so I wouldn't have to think about losing Sophie that night in the earthquake.

"I'm glad to see you and Lucian together," Georgina said between chip crunches.

I smiled. "I've missed him, too."

She looked at me for a long moment. "Are you in love with him?"

"Yeah probably." I chuckled.

"No, I meant Hades."

I sobered a little, but said wistfully, "Yeah probably."

"You're different around him."

"I'm aware." I laid on the bed. "It's just he makes me feel things that I don't feel with anyone else."

"Like what?"

"Strong. Fierce. Powerful. Like I could pick a fight with the world and win."

"Lucian doesn't make you feel those things."

I rolled onto my side and looked at her. "No, but he makes me feel strong in other ways. Like I'm important. Does that make sense?"

She laid on her side as well, propped up on her elbow. "I don't know. It's not like I understand guys at all."

I narrowed my eyes. "I have a feeling there's a story in there you're not telling me."

She shook her head, but I caught the shy smile. "Ha! Not a story at all. A paragraph maybe."

"Uh-huh, what's his name?"

"Everett."

I made a face thinking. "Isn't he that really stalky guy with the longish brown hair. He wears it in a ponytail."

She nodded shyly.

"Oh, he's cute. Well done, Gina."

She shook her head. "He's not my boyfriend or anything. We've just, had a few…moments."

I laughed. "Moments. Uh-huh. Like kissing moments?"

She tossed her pillow at me. "Shut up."

I tossed it back, and we started talking about other things. By the time we both rolled over to sleep, I was feeling lighter. Georgina had taken the weight off my shoulders. I knew it was temporary, but I appreciated the reprieve her friendship had given me.

An hour later, I heard Georgina's soft snores. Although my body was beyond exhausted, I couldn't sleep. I had too much on my mind. I sat up and decided a short walk through the hall might spend the rest of this nervous energy.

Everyone must've also been asleep, as I was alone in the hall. I walked through the meandering paths around the plants and lagoons. I found a door that led to an outdoor garden and decided some air would probably do me some good.

The moment I went outside, the skunky scent of weed hit me in the face. I walked around the corner to find Demeter sitting cross-legged on the grass smoking. She coughed on her next hit when she spotted me.

"Melany. You startled me."

"I'm sorry, I'll just go."

She lifted her hand toward me. "No, don't. Come and sit with me." I did and she offered me a hit. "I know I shouldn't offer it to the students, but you know what, you're an adult. You're perfectly capable of making decisions for yourself."

I shook my head. "No thanks."

Demeter took another hit, then snuffed it out. "Fun night, huh?"

I snorted. "Yup, can't remember a better ceremony."

"Dionysus didn't poison you."

"I know. I think it's ridiculous that he was taken or arrested, or whatever happened."

She leaned back onto her elbows on the grass.

"Makes sense though, as he's the poison master and the wine maker."

"Lucian told me he overheard someone planning to kill me."

She frowned. "When? Who?"

"When he was recovering in the infirmary. He didn't know who it was."

She nodded. "Ah. So there is a small list of suspects. I'd be on that list."

"I don't think you want to kill me."

"No?" She smiled. "And why not?"

"You're way too chill."

She guffawed, then choked on her laughter. "That's good. I like that." She sobered, then regarded me. "So, who do you think it was?"

"Aphrodite for sure. I suspect she is planning something with Ares. Twice now I've heard them conspiring, and twice now I've found golden rope near sites of disasters."

She frowned. "I know about the earthquake, but—"

Hades would kill me if he knew I was about to tell her what happened to us, but I knew I could trust Demeter. There was something about her that made me feel secure, something familiar. "Hades and I encountered Oceanus in Nice the other night."

She sat up. "What happened?"

"He started to flood the city. We attacked him, and I saw there was a golden cord around his neck. When I cut it off, he came to his senses. He wasn't sure how he got there or who put the rope around his throat."

"Have you told Zeus?"

I shook my head. "Hades didn't want to. In fact, he'd probably be pissed that I told you. But I'm tired of being told what to do. He hasn't been completely truthful with me, either."

Demeter gave me a side-eyed glance. "None of the Gods are completely truthful."

"Not even you?"

She rubbed at her face. "Nope, not even me. We have thousands of years of practice of twisting the truth. It becomes as natural as breathing."

I studied her profile. "I met Persephone."

She turned her head then to look at me. "How?"

"When I died. She met me in Elysium."

She nodded. "That makes sense."

"Why? Who is she? What does she have to do with me? With Hades? Just tell me one truth. I'm tired of everyone lying."

"Here's your one truth Melany Richmond. You are a direct descendant of Persephone. You have her blood in your veins. And you have my blood in your veins."

I gaped at her as a heavy feeling filled my stomach.

"Persephone is my daughter."

I sprang to my feet, too anxious to sit still. "But, if that's true, why don't I have powerful earth abilities? Why am I not a part of your clan?"

She also stood, as I paced around her. "You do have powerful earth abilities and water and fire and electric. But it's your affinity to the darkness that holds you sway. It's what seduced Persephone and took her from me."

"You mean Hades."

"Yes, but he and the darkness are one in the same." She reached for me. "And I know he's seduced you, too. It reads all over you."

I pulled away from her touch. I didn't want it right now. "I think you're wrong about Hades taking Persephone. I think she went willingly." I searched my own mind, my heart, my soul, and I knew that I had gone willingly. "She told me to tell Hades that she didn't leave him. That she was taken away from him against her will. She didn't have time to say, but I'm sure Zeus had something to do with it."

Demeter shook her head, as if she didn't want to hear the truth. I supposed after thousands of years of lies and mistruths, that honesty was like a slap in the face.

"She told me other things as well. About a war, that I would be the one to end it."

The Goddess grabbed my hands, forcing me to look her in the eye. "There is so much you need to know, and I don't know how to tell you, or what to tell you. If Persephone has indeed prophesized this, then you must know the truth."

"Then tell me."

"Go into the maze. There you will find a portal that will lead you to the Hall of Knowledge and everything you will ever need—"

"Am I interrupting?"

I swung around to see Aphrodite walking across the garden toward us.

Demeter dropped my hands and stepped away from me. "Melany and I were just having a little girl time."

"I'm sorry I'm late for our meeting, Demeter. I had a few things to take care of, as I'm sure you know." Her smile was full of maliciousness, and I wanted to scratch it off her.

I glanced at Demeter, but she gave nothing away. Could I even trust her? Now, I didn't know.

Aphrodite looked me over. "You look pretty lively for someone who died."

I took a step toward her. "I'm surprised you care."

"Oh, I don't."

"Go back to the dorm, Melany," Demeter warned. "Get some sleep. You've had a long eventful day."

I considered mounting an attack on Aphrodite, but I was still exhausted, my body still not fully healed. It would be foolish to do so, as it would just give her an excuse to kill me in self defense. No, I had to gather my strength, and my will, as I knew that one day soon, we would be on opposite sides of a battle, facing each other, and I'd need everything I had to defeat her.

CHAPTER TWELVE

MELANY

I managed to get a few hours of sleep when I returned to Georgina's room. She was still asleep when I tiptoed back in thankfully, so I didn't have to explain where I'd been or what happened. Everything was still swirling around in my head when I woke up. I still wasn't sure how to sort out my emotions about what I'd learned.

I wanted to trust Demeter, everything inside told me I could, but her meeting with Aphrodite gave me pause. Especially since Aphrodite seemed smug about it. Although she always appeared smug, so maybe it was just my paranoia getting the better of me.

My stomach rumbled loudly, so I was happy to accompany Georgina to the dining hall. I still wore the clothes she gave me; I didn't think my dress would be appropriate early morning breakfast wear. There was a lot of mumbling and whispering when I entered the room. I ignored it and got in line to get some eggs, bacon, and toast. Some of my peers visibly flinched as I neared. Did they think I was cursed or something? Or I had some disease that could be transmitted?

As I carried my tray to the table where Ren, Mia, Rosie, and Marek sat, I heard some of the whispers buzzing around.

"I can't believe she'd blame Jasmine."

"Jasmine wouldn't hurt anyone."

"I heard they were fighting over Lucian."

"I heard it was over Hades."

"She's such a slut. Did you see the dress she wore?"

"She totally had sex with Hades."

"Yeah, but who wouldn't? He's hot."

"Poor Lucian. He so doesn't deserve her bullshit."

"I wish Lucian hadn't saved her."

I sat at the table, the urge to cry and the urge to punch someone in the face battling for supremacy in my head. No one at the table said much to me except for a brief greeting, which also hurt. I started to eat, but I could still hear the whispers. They were getting louder and bolder and painful.

I set down my fork, stood, stepped up onto the seat, then onto the table. I turned to address the room. "I didn't arrest Jasmine. I know she wouldn't hurt me. No, we weren't fighting over Lucian or Hades. Jasmine has a very nice girlfriend named Mia. I'm sorry if my dress made you uncomfortable, but I looked hella good in it.

It's none of your Gods damn business if I had sex with Hades! I'm an adult I can do what I want. And, bitches, I am alive and well. So, get used to it!"

Every face turned my way looked surprised. Including Lucian's, who I hadn't noticed had come into the room. I'd wished he hadn't heard any of that.

Georgina stood and clapped. "Well said."

I got down from the table just as Lucian came over. "What was that all about?"

"Some things I had to get off my chest."

He didn't look happy. I imagined hearing about the possibility of me having sex with Hades bright and early in the morning wasn't the best wake-up call. I'm sorry it had come out at all, as I didn't want to hurt him.

"Do you still want to see Jasmine?"

"Yes, of course I do."

"Then we need to go now."

Georgina hugged me. "I'll see you later. You can crash with me again if you need to."

"Thanks."

I followed Lucian out of the dining hall to the main foyer, around the corner and down the spiraling stone steps.

"We're going to the forge?"

"Hephaistos is going to help us."

"How?"

"He's the one who built the cells. He devised a back way inside."

We went into the forge and found Hephaistos

shaping a piece of metal into what I was sure was a new sword. I noticed he had several new swords in various stages of creation. He set the metal into the cooling bucket, then pushed up his face protector to look at us.

"Thank you for helping us," I said.

"I'm doing it for the academy and the cadets. I don't like what's being going on behind closed doors." He gave me a death glare as if I was the one causing the problems. Then he mumbled under his breath. "I should never have gotten involved."

I frowned. "What do you mean? How are you involved with this, with me?"

"Stop pestering me. There's been no peace since you arrived."

"Hey, that's not my fault. I'm not the one trying to kill me."

"I know, girl. Don't get all riled up. I've just prided myself on staying out of the bullshit politics."

I so wanted to ask him about the bullshit politics he was trying to stay out of, but I knew he wouldn't discuss it. Hephaistos was the strong, silent, grumpy type. Emphasis on grumpy.

He set his tools down and motioned for us to follow him. He led us across the bridge, down a set of stairs, over another bridge that crested the river of molten metal, and to a stone wall in a darkened corner. Mind you, all the corners here were dark.

Hephaistos ran his hand along the wall, then one of the stones moved, and he pulled it out, handed it to

Lucian then stuck his hand into the hole, and the stone slid away to reveal a dark passage.

"At the end of the passage, take a right, you'll come to a locked door. Use fire to open it."

We stepped into the tunnel.

"Oh, you'll have to find another way out. You can't come back this way. No one can know I helped you."

I met his gaze. "You know one day soon you're going to have to take a stand. A war is coming, Hephaistos. You can't hide in your forge forever."

Without a word, he slid the wall shut, plunging us into complete darkness.

A few seconds later, we both formed fire balls in our hands so we could see.

"You have a funny way of thanking people for their help," Lucian said.

I frowned at him as we moved down the passage. I had a feeling he wasn't just talking about Hephaistos. "You're right. I never truly thanked you for saving my life."

"I wasn't talking about that."

I set my hand on his arm and got him to look at me. "Thank you. You've saved me in multiple ways."

He caressed my face. "I'd do it again without hesitation."

"Good, because I have a feeling that won't be the last time someone tries to kill me." I smirked.

"Well, you do seem innately skilled in making enemies."

"It's because I'm so damn charming."

He laughed, and we continued on our way.

At the end of the passage, we took a right and almost immediately came to a locked wooden door. Lucian examined it, frowning.

"Knowing Hephaistos, it will take some kind of fancy fire and smoke to find a way to open it."

"Yeah, we don't have time for that." I set my hand on the door handle and created a fire so hot that in seconds the metal reddened like hot coals then started to melt. The result was a hole in the door and a destroyed locking mechanism. I put my hand through the hole and easily pushed the door open.

Lucian shook his head. "There goes our sneaking in advantage."

I shrugged, then peered around the corner into a long empty corridor dug out of the stone with curved archways. I had no idea where the cells were or if there were guards. For the most part, we were operating on blind faith that we were going to get away with this.

Before we went marching through the prison, I grabbed Lucian's hand and gathered the shadows around us for camouflage. If we did happen to run into anyone, we'd be practically invisible to them. Together we ventured out into the corridor.

I led the way, Lucian right behind me. We passed a couple of empty cells. The crisscrossed bars were thick iron. Then I stopped in front of one, eyes focusing on a dark form in the corner lying on the floor. I stepped out of the shadows and went to the bars.

"Jasmine?"

The form looked up. I could see then that it was indeed my friend. She stood, stumbled, then came to the bars. I nearly wept to see that she'd been hurt. There weren't obvious bruises on her face, but I spotted the scorch marks on her hands and feet, where I imagined electric bolts had been used.

I reached my hands through the bars and took hold of her arm, careful not to harm her. "I'm going to kill whoever did this to you."

"They tortured you?" Lucian's voice was incredulous. I wasn't sure why he sounded so surprised. They'd been torturing all of us in the name of training. In the trials, they even pitted us against each other to see who could endure the most torture.

Jasmine nodded. "They kept asking what side I was on."

"Why would they ask you that?" Lucian asked.

She shrugged and sobbed. "I don't know."

I pulled her closer to the bars, so I could cup her face. "I'm so sorry, Jas. This is all my fault."

"How? You were the one poisoned."

"This is about more than an attempt on my life. There are factions being developed in the academy. I think the Gods are starting to pick sides."

"For what?" she asked.

"A war."

"Over what?" Lucian asked.

"I think over the academy itself."

"That doesn't make sense," Jasmine said.

"I'm not sure, but Demeter told me to find a place

under the maze that would tell me everything I need to know." I pulled back and wrapped my hands around the bars. "But first I'm getting you out of here. Stand back. I'm going to melt these bars."

"I tried that," Jasmine said as she stepped back. "It doesn't work. I think our powers are muted in here."

Concentrating on the metal, I pushed all my kinetic energy into my hands. Flames erupted over my fingers, curling up to my wrists. I could feel the fire burning, but it wasn't having any effect on the bars. They remained black and cold.

"Lucian, put her hands over mine and direct your lightning into them."

"What if I electrocute you?"

"I handled Zeus's bolt, remember?"

He did as I asked and settled his hands over mine on the bars. Within seconds, I could see the sparks zipping off his hands. An electrical current shot over my fingers and up my arms. The pain was immediate and sharp, and I gritted my teeth, but I refused to let go of the bars. But after a few minutes, the metal still wasn't heating up and most definitely wasn't melting.

"Damn it." I released my grip on the bars, and Lucian dropped his hands.

"What are you doing here?"

I whirled around to see two guards, wearing leather armor and carrying spears, running down the passageway toward us.

For a brief second, I considered tossing some fire balls at them, but the last thing we needed was a battle that wasn't going to get us anywhere except possibly thrown in the cell next to Jasmine.

"I want to see Zeus," I demanded.

I didn't think the guards were expecting that because they looked at each other curiously.

Fifteen minutes later, we were escorted up to Zeus's private chambers. It helped that Lucian was part of his clan because the guards didn't argue with us. He had access to the hall anyway.

Zeus greeted us with a warm smile. "Melany, it's good to see you up and about. How are you feeling?"

"I'm fine, thanks to Lucian."

Zeus beamed at Lucian and put his hand on Lucian's shoulder, like a father to a son. "Yes, quite heroic. I had no idea you possessed that kind of power."

"Nor did I," Lucian said. I could see that he looked a bit uncomfortable.

"Well, it worked out for the best." He moved away from us, his long white robe dragging on the floor behind him.

"I want Jasmine released. She had nothing to do with poisoning me."

"Technically, she did. She gave you the glass of wine."

"She was used. She didn't know that the wine was poisoned."

"Yes, I surmised that. She has no motive for your murder." Zeus waved his hand. "She will be released."

"When?"

He turned, and I saw the annoyed sparks in his eyes.

Lucian grabbed my hand and squeezed it in warning. "Thank you, Zeus," he said.

I refused to thank him, as Jasmine shouldn't have been detained to begin with, but Lucian nudged me in the side.

"Yeah, thank you." I figured it wouldn't hurt to keep the all-powerful God on my side.

He walked toward us again, his brow furrowed. "I didn't realize the two of you were close. An item? Is that what the term is?"

"We're good friends," I said. "Strong allies."

Zeus nodded. "That's good. It's important to have…friends here. The academy and the training we do can be a very isolating thing for cadets. Especially when one stands out among the others. Sometimes friends are hard to keep."

I had a sense there was a warning in there somewhere. But I wasn't sure to whom. Me or Lucian?

CHAPTER THIRTEEN

MELANY

*a*fter we left Zeus's hall, Lucian suggested we go flying together like we used to before all the shit happened, before the trials, before Hades. We went outside toward the maze to unfurl our wings. I pushed mine out, a tension in my back releasing, and spread them out around me. Shivers rushed over my body at the anticipation of taking flight. I smiled at Lucian then took off into the sky.

I'd forgotten how it felt to soar through the open air. For the past few months, all my flying had been done in the training room in Hades's Hall. This was freeing in more ways than one. Laughing, I did a corkscrew up, then dove back down toward the ground, swooping up at the last moment. That move always made my belly flip over.

Lucian flew in beside me, and we swooped toward the woods and lake. Together, we soared over the tree-tops. I lowered my hand and brushed my fingers against the highest branch of leaves. Then we glided over the lake. I stared at our reflection in the water, watching as my black wings flapped, the tips touching the water, and Lucian's beautiful red ones doing the same. We made quite the impressive pair.

After flying over the lake a bunch of times, we jetted back to our favorite spot—the top of the tallest tower of the academy. Once I landed, I folded in my wings and walked to the edge to look out over the grounds. I could see the training field, the maze, and the cobblestone path to the academy that I remembered walking when I first arrived. I couldn't believe how much had changed since then.

Lucian came up to my side. "The view from up here will always be awesome."

I nodded. "Yeah. I've missed it."

"I've missed you." He grabbed my hand.

"I've missed you, too."

"Have you?"

I turned to him. I knew what he was really asking me. Hearing about Hades this morning must've been hurtful. I wanted to tell him that being with Hades hadn't meant anything, that I didn't have feelings for him, but that would be a lie. I had very real, very strong emotions for the God of darkness, just as I had feelings for Lucian.

I reached up and traced my hand over his brow,

down his cheek to his lips. He kissed the tips of my fingers. I stepped into him, wrapping my other hand around his waist. Slowly, he dipped his head down and pressed his lips to mine.

My heart leapt into my throat as he cupped me around the neck and deepened the kiss. Holding me tight, he walked me back into the stone turret wall. His face nuzzled my neck, then he brushed his lips over my chin, then up to my mouth again. He swept his tongue over mine.

A little moan escaped my throat. I couldn't stop it. I was too swept up in what he was doing to me with his kiss. My body was on fire for him. I fisted my hands in his shirt and kissed him back just as hard, just as frantic.

His hands moved down to my waist, his thumbs pressed into my hips. My belly fluttered. Then that flutter lowered between my legs, and I moaned again. Louder this time. I couldn't keep it in. I wanted Lucian so bad.

Pulling back, he rested his forehead against mine, his breath coming in short hard gasps. His thumbs were still pressed into my hips, and I so desperately wanted them to slide down lower, to be bolder.

"I don't want to stop this time," he murmured.

My throat was dry, but I managed to say, "Then don't."

Covering my mouth with his again, his hands moved upward, slipping under my shirt. He palmed my breasts, and I gasped in pleasure. As he tweaked my nipples with his fingers, he nibbled on my bottom lip, then pressed kisses to my chin, over my neck to my ear. With his tongue, he made little circles just under my earlobe. A pleasant shiver rippled over my skin.

Heat rushed over my entire body as he lifted my shirt to expose my breasts to the cool air. Lowering his head, he pressed his lips to one nipple, then licked it with his tongue. I gasped, as he moved over and lavished the same attention on my other breast.

I was burning up. I didn't think I could stand his delicious teasing. My hands raced down to the waist-band of his pants and unbuttoned them. Once undone, I slid a hand down and over his erection. He groaned against my skin, the rumble of it sending a rush of shivers over my belly and straight down between my legs.

He pulled back, and I thought he was going to tell me this wasn't a good idea, or we shouldn't, or some shit like that.

He rested his head against mine. "Not here. I don't want to take you against this wall out in the open where anyone can see us." He did up his pants, and the grabbed my hand. "C'mon."

Together, we lifted into the air, and Lucian guided us to another tower, to one of the windows. He pushed it open and climbed inside. I followed him to see it was his room in Zeus's Hall. Still holding my hand, he led me to his bed.

He guided my arms up over my head and pulled off my shirt. His gaze swept over me, there was a hunger in his eyes, but also appreciation and love. I scooted back onto his bed and lay back as he knelt beside me and hooked his fingers into the waistband of my sweatpants and slowly drew them off.

Then I was completely naked lying on his bed, but I didn't feel exposed or vulnerable. I was proud of my body even with its tattoos and scars, and Lucian's admiring scan of me sent heat blossoming all over. He got off the bed and quickly took off his own clothes. I watched him, enjoying the sight of his powerful yet lean body. He was beautiful to look at. Then he lay beside me on the bed and began his exploration.

He touched and kissed every part of me. He trailed his tongue along the branches of lightning that marred the side of my neck and down my side. His slow worship of my body turned me into a quivering hot mess. Then I couldn't stand it anymore. I needed him to be inside me. I craved release and only Lucian could give it to me.

I reached for him, burying my hands in his silky golden waves, and pulled him down. He positioned himself between my parted legs, and I could see the restraint he used to stop from completely losing himself. But I wanted to see him lose control. I needed him to.

"You won't hurt me," I said as I hooked my legs around his waist. "I'm not fragile."

"I know." He leaned down and kissed me. "But you deserve to be worshipped."

Then finally, blissfully, he guided himself between my legs and in one quick thrust was inside me. I cried out as my body squeezed around him. A tsunami of heat surged over us, and we were swept away by it.

Then it was all panic and heat and hunger as our bodies melded together.

It wasn't long before I lost all control and came, digging my fingers into his back and crying out.

Collapsing on top of me, Lucian buried his face into the side of my neck and followed me over the edge of orgasm.

After his body ceased quivering, he rolled over onto his back. We were both sweaty and breathing hard. It felt like I'd been through a three-hour workout. My heart was still racing. Eventually, I turned my head to look at Lucian. His eyes were closed, and he had a wide silly grin on his face. It made me giggle. I never giggled.

His eyes opened and he turned to look at me. "That was incredible. I feel like I could dead lift the world with one hand."

"Ha! You'll be asleep in fifteen minutes, I bet."

"Nope." He reached for me and rolled me up onto his chest. Then he lifted me up into the air. "See!"

I squealed. "But I'm not the world."

He lowered me down and wrapped his arms around me. "You're my world."

I pushed up onto my elbows and looked into his eyes. His love for me was evident, and I swallowed against the well of emotions flooding inside of me. I feathered my fingers over his face, his nose, his cheeks, his chin, his lips, memorizing each part of him. My feelings for him were huge, but I didn't know how to express them in a way that he'd know how much he meant to me. How important he was.

"I'm scared that I'm going to lose you."

He tucked some hair behind my ear. "You're never going to lose me, Blue. No matter what happens I'll always be there for you."

"Why? I'm not a good person."

He smiled and searched my face. "You're better than you'll ever know."

I shook my head. "I've done some things…Hades and I—"

"I see the darkness in you. I know it's a part of who you are, and I don't care." He cupped my cheek with his hand. "I love you for who you are, not for who you think you should be to make other people happy."

"But it's not fair to you."

"I'm a big boy. Let me decide what's fair or not."

Tears slipped down my cheeks. I didn't deserve this man. He had a heart of gold and a soul to match. Maybe that was why we fit together. His light complimented my darkness. Together we made sense.

I leaned forward and pressed my lips to his. He brought his hands up to my hair. Deepening the kiss, he rolled me over onto my back, and for the next couple of hours we just loved each other in the best possible ways we could.

Afterward, we slept. Well, Lucian slept. I laid on my back staring up at the ceiling. There were too many thoughts whirling around in my mind. I needed to get under the maze and find the room Demeter told me about where I'd find answers. War was coming, and I needed to be fully prepared. I needed to know who I was fighting against and who I was fighting for and what the outcome was meant to be.

As silently as I could, I got out of the bed and found my clothes. I quickly put them on but felt greatly underdressed for an adventure underground in only a pair of sweatpants and thin T-shirt. I opened Lucian's closet and found training gear much like I wore in the underworld. I didn't think he'd mind if I borrowed a pair of pants and a long-sleeved shirt and socks. I'd have to make do with the sneakers that Georgina had lent me as Lucian's boot would be too big.

I also pilfered one of his knives he had stashed away. I took it and a holder that wrapped around my leg. I got outfitted, then after a long look at Lucian still sleeping, I gathered the shadows around me, and zipped down to the maze.

CHAPTER FOURTEEN

MELANY

I stepped out of the shadows right beside the gazebo in the middle of the maze. Thankfully, no one else was here. I found that not a lot of my fellow cadets came into the maze. There were rumors that it was haunted by Medusa's ex-lovers who she'd turned to stone. I assumed they thought all the stone statues outside and around the maze were once people. I was pretty sure those rumors were started because everyone was afraid of the snake-haired demigoddess. Not that I didn't blame them. She was frightening, but I kind of liked that about her.

I stepped up into the gazebo and looked around. Demeter had said I'd find a door in the maze. She didn't necessarily say in the gazebo, but where else could there be a door? I needed more light as the sun was setting, casting darker and deeper shadows around the hedges. For a moment, I considered stepping into them to return to Hades, but I was still angry at him. And with Lucian's scent still on my skin, his taste on my tongue, I didn't want to rub me and Lucian's reunion in his face. Not that I thought he'd care.

I held my hand over one of the four big cauldrons set around the gazebo and set it ablaze with fire. I did the same with the other three. Just as I finished lighting the last one, I sensed movement behind me. I unsheathed the dagger on my leg and swung around, my arm up in defense.

Georgina yelped. "Don't stab me. I like my insides where they belong—inside my body."

Sighing, I lowered my weapon and shook my head at her and Lucian, who had come up behind her. "The both of you move too quietly."

"So do you or I would've woken when you snuck out of my room."

I blushed a little since Georgina was there and probably knew what we'd been doing in his room. "You looked too peaceful to wake."

His lips twitched up as he did a once over. "Are you wearing my clothes?"

I shrugged. "Yes. The T-shirt and sweatpants I had weren't up to code for an adventure."

"They look good." There was a humor-filled glint in his eyes.

My eyes narrowed. "How did you know where I was?"

"When I woke, saw that you were gone, I figured you were up to something. So I tracked Georgina down, thinking maybe you might have told her something. She didn't really know but knew you'd talked to Demeter."

"She told you I'd be here?"

He nodded. "When are you going to learn that you don't have to do these things on your own?"

I shrugged. "Probably never." I chuckled.

"What are we looking for?" Georgina asked.

"A door of some kind."

"Well, we can probably assume it's not going to be some ordinary door," Lucian said as he inspected the floor of the gazebo.

"Did she say door?" Georgina asked.

I stopped to think for a moment. "Hmm, I think she said portal actually."

"Okay, tell me exactly what she said." Georgina put her hands on her hips and gave me a look.

I closed my eyes for a second to recollect the conversation I had with Demeter. "She said…go to the maze. There you will find a portal to the Hall of Knowledge and—"

"Hall of Knowledge, are you sure?"

I nodded. "Yes."

"I think I know where the portal is." Georgina took off into the maze.

Lucian and I followed her, having no choice. Because it was dark, I created a ball of fire to give us some light. After a few twists and turns in the maze,

Georgina stopped in front of one of the stone statues. I came closer to see that it was of an owl and not a man.

"Okay? What are we supposed to be seeing?" I asked her.

"Whose symbol is the owl?"

"Athena," Lucian answered.

"And what is she the goddess of?"

"Wisdom." I slung my arm around her shoulders. "You're a genius, Gina."

"No, I just listened during history of the Gods class while you were daydreaming about fighting hydras and minotaurs."

I scrutinized the owl statute. "Okay, so how do we get this to work?" I reached for it and tried to pry it off the stone pillar it sat on. It didn't budge. Then I tried pushing the whole thing over thinking there'd be some kind of secret entrance underneath. That didn't work, either.

I stepped back and looked at the stone statue again. "What do we know about owls and Athena?"

"The owl is said to be the Goddess's companion. It's supposed to help her see all," Georgina said.

See all? How do owls see? With their eyes. I crouched down to look at the stone bird's face. The flames from my hand flickered over the statue to reveal two large round orbs where its eyes would be. I looked at my hand again, and the light of the fire. Owls could see in the dark.

I put my other hand over the fire and snuffed it out.

"What are you doing?" Lucian asked.

The moment we were plunged into darkness, light glowed from the owl's eyes. I looked into it but didn't see anything. Then I stood back and saw that the light made twin beams that shot forward.

"Move out of its way." I pulled Lucian aside, and we stood beside the statue.

Then I saw a pool of light hovering in the air about six feet from the statue. When I moved, it glimmered.

"It's a portal," Georgina said in awe.

One by one, we walked toward the shimmer in the air. I stuck my hand into the pool of light. A prickling sensation went up my arm as my hand disappeared. I pulled it out again to make sure it was still intact, and I hadn't disintegrated.

"Fortune favors the brave." I took in a deep breath then stepped into the glimmering portal.

I immediately appeared in a circular room, made from marble with giant pillars and a domed prettily painted ceiling. There were several lit torches in sconces around the room. The warm orange glow illuminated shelves upon shelves of rolled scrolls and large yellowing tomes. The place looked old. Not just old but ancient.

Lucian and Georgina appeared beside me. "Wow, it's a library," Georgina said as she gaped at the surroundings. "*The* library. The Library of the Gods."

Lucian ran his hand over one of the pillars. "What are we supposed to be looking for?"

"My parents said to look into the past of the academy. That I would find answers."

Surprised, Lucian whirled toward me. "Your parents? I thought they died when you were young."

"They did. But I saw them when I died and went to Elysium." I moved toward one of the shelves and pulled out one of the scrolls.

"Mel, I think there's a bunch of stuff you haven't told us."

I proceeded to tell Lucian and Georgina about being in Elysium and meeting Persephone and my parents and what they told me. I also told them about what Demeter had told me as well about my connection to Persephone and to herself.

"Whoa." Georgina looked stunned. "Demeter is like your great-great-great-great-great times hundred grandmother."

I shook my head. "I don't think it works like that."

"I don't know. I think it does. You have her blood running through your veins. As do I, that's why I'm in her clan and have an affinity to the earth. So technically we're like sisters." Laughing, she grabbed my arm and pulled me in for a hug.

I hugged her back, shaking my head.

"So, we're looking for anything about the history of the academy?" Lucian asked.

I nodded, then we got to work.

I wasn't sure how long we pulled out scrolls, unrolled them, read them, and put them back, but it was most definitely hours. I'd just gotten my third papercut on the skin between my thumb and index finger, when Lucian called out from the far side of the library.

"I found something."

Georgina and I gathered around him and the scroll he had rolled out on one of the stone tables. He pointed to a paragraph of text. "It says that the academy was founded in 700 BC."

"Whoa. I didn't think it was that old. Our history texts say that the academy was created during the New Dawn in the early 1900s to protect the world from the Titans." Georgina shook her head. "Why would the historians lie about that?"

"I'm pretty sure it wasn't the historians who were lying. They can only write about what they know to be true," I said.

"There's more," Lucian said. "The academy was founded by Prometheus and Hesiod as a place for higher learning for Gods and humans alike."

I couldn't believe it. This was what Hades had been alluding to, when he said that the academy didn't belong to Zeus.

"Holy crap," Georgina sighed. "Prometheus was a Titan. The story goes he gave fire to mortals and cared for their wellbeing. And the rumor is that Zeus didn't like that Prometheus favored mortals over the Gods, and, therefore, cursed Prometheus to an eternity of torture."

"Why would the Gods lie about the nature of the academy?" Lucian asked.

"Because it's no longer a place of learning but a

place to learn to fight and kill." I rubbed at the scar on my cheek. It was throbbing a little, as a reminder of Zeus's penchant for torture.

"But to fight against the Titans, right? To keep the world safe." Georgina frowned.

"Are we so sure now that it's the Titans who are a threat to our world?" I stormed back to the shelves and pulled out more scrolls and books. "There has to be more here. My parents said they were part of the academy. They said they were killed protecting me."

"Protecting you from what?" Lucian rolled up the scroll.

"From who, maybe." I flipped through the giant tome I pulled from the shelf. "Someone is trying to kill me."

"To keep you from being 'the one to end the war?'" Lucian came to my side.

I shrugged. "Yeah, maybe. I don't know." I continued to flip pages.

"Do you still think it's Aphrodite and Ares?" he asked.

I swallowed and shook my head. "I'm starting to think maybe it's bigger than the two of them."

He frowned. "You can't possibly think—"

"I don't know. He's the head of the academy. He's the all-knowing, the all-powerful. I can't imagine anything goes on without his knowledge." Then, I found the information I was looking for.

Right there staring at me was a photo, a recent one by the looks of it, maybe ten years old. It was of my parents. They were smiling, they looked happy, and standing between them with his arms over their shoulders was Zeus.

They had been part of the academy, and Zeus had known them both.

I pushed away from the table, my heart racing. My throat went dry and I found it hard to breathe.

"Holy shit." Lucian stared down at the picture. "Is that your parents?"

I nodded but pulled at the collar of my shirt. I couldn't get any air.

Georgina rushed toward me and rubbed a hand over my back. She bent me over. "Take a deep breath, then let it out slowly."

I did as she instructed. It was helping even though my heart felt like it was going to burst out of my throat.

"I can't believe this." Lucian started to pace the room, rubbing at his face. "It's all been a bunch of lies."

I straightened and rubbed at my mouth. Georgina still ran a hand up and down my back to soothe me. I was about to say what we should do about the information we'd obtained when something out of the corner of my eye drew my attention.

I swirled around just as one of the stone statues from the maze came through the portal. And he was holding a sword and a shield.

CHAPTER FIFTEEN

MELANY

"I think we have a problem."

Lucian and Georgina looked to where I pointed as three more stone soldiers armed with weapons came through the portal.

"It must be a security system for the library," Georgina said.

"You'd think it would've been activated the moment we got inside, not hours later." I unsheathed my dagger, although I wasn't sure it would be any good against stone. "No, I think this is something else."

By the time we lined up side by side, two more stone statues entered the library. There were now six of them in front of us, blocking our exit. I didn't know if they were here to detain us or kill us, and I supposed it didn't matter. One was as bad as the other in my opinion.

"Can you shadow us out of here?" Lucian asked.

I shook my head. I'd already tested the shadows, and they were blocked. We couldn't travel through them. I wasn't surprised though because I didn't even know where the library truly was. We could've been anywhere. Underneath the academy or a thousand miles away, maybe even another dimension parallel to this one. It was hard to know. Nothing about coming to the academy to train had been comprehensible. It had all been cloaked in secrecy and lies.

"Maybe I can reason with them."

"They're made of stone, Gina. It's not like they have fully functioning brains."

Georgina stepped toward the soldiers. "We didn't come here to steal anything." She took another step forward with her hands out to prove she wasn't a threat.

One of the stone statues carrying a spear and shield, moved forward, while advancing its spear. Georgina had to back up to avoid being poked in the chest with the tip.

"Okay. I guess that didn't work." She moved back to stand with us.

"This is crap." I took a few steps forward. "Let us pass. Now."

They all moved like they were preparing to attack. I didn't like this situation one bit.

I sheathed my dagger, then gathered the shadows to

me. Although I couldn't use them for travel, I could use them to make a weapon just as Hades had when we fought Oceanus. I wrapped my hands around the darkness and drew them upward like the way I'd seen Hades do it. It took a couple of tries, but eventually I managed to fashion a short shadow sword.

"What are you doing?" Lucian asked.

"Getting us out of here." I lifted the sword into a ready position. "Use your lightning to blast them."

"Maybe we should wait to see who—" Georgina started.

"It doesn't matter who sent them. We're going to be detained just like Jasmine. I refuse to be anyone's prisoner."

I advanced on the soldiers, expecting that Lucian and Georgina were behind me ready to attack. The statue in the middle with the sword came at me. He swung toward my head, but because of his bulkiness, his aim was off, and I was able to duck under it, and then come up with my sword. The shadow blade struck the statue across the chest. It didn't do what I had hoped, but I was rewarded with a fissure across the stone. A few more hits like that, and the solider would crumble.

Lucian blasted the soldier with the spear, breaking the weapon in half. It fell to the floor and shattered into pieces. Georgina managed to pick up one of the pedestals that were scattered decoratively around the library and threw it at the soldiers. It broke across one soldier's helmet and managed to chip off a few pieces of its face. When it turned toward her, to attack, I saw that it no longer had a nose. Score one for Georgina.

I wanted to turn toward her and give her a high five but thought maybe it wasn't prudent in the middle of a battle. I grinned instead. If we kept hacking away at them piece by piece, we'd definitely win.

The swordsman came at me again, backing me up into the marble table. I leapt onto the table just as it swung its sword. I jumped over the blade. The air vibrated just under my feet as it whizzed by me. The sword came down on the table and cracked it in half. I kicked the statue in the head, it didn't do any damage, except maybe to my big toe, but the blow got its attention. As it turned toward me, I curved my shadow sword toward its midsection and swung.

When my blade hit the stone, it vibrated up over my arms. It nearly rattled my teeth, but I hit my mark, and the stone solider cracked in half, the two pieces falling to the floor, where it broke even more. One down, five to go.

Two of the soldiers advanced on Lucian. He sent another blast of lightning at one, as he ducked under the other's spear as it was thrust at him. The bolt did the job and cracked the solider along the midsection and arm. It would take one blow to shatter it into pieces. I tossed my shadow sword to Lucian, as I attempted to make another one while running.

Lucian swung at the spearman, aiming for the visible fracture, and hit the target. The soldier's arm broke off and shattered on the floor. The rest of it crumbled into pieces as it tried another attack at Lucian.

Georgina got cornered by the other two statues. She'd run out of podiums and heavy stone vases to toss at them.

"Use your earth powers, Gina! You're stronger than they are!" I shouted at her as one solider drew back with his sword and was about to cut her across the shoulder.

She caught the sword in her hands. It was amazing. Then she proceeded to squeeze it in her grip. I could hear the stone breaking apart from where I launched an attack on the last two soldiers guarding the portal. It was time to bail and get out of the library. Once we were out, I could jump us into a shadow and get us somewhere safe.

I hit one of the stone guards in the shoulder, cracking its armor. It stumbled sideways giving us a very small window of opportunity.

"Get to the portal!"

Lucian ran toward Georgina, sent a blast of lightning at the last soldier near her, then grabbed her hand and pulled her toward the portal. I was already on my way there but stopped. I wasn't leaving without some sort of proof of the lies Zeus and the others had been telling. I rushed back to the broken table, snatched the big tome, hugged it to my chest, and ran back to the glimmering doorway. I swung my shadow sword at the other stone statue as it turned toward me. The black blade hit it in the head and took it clean off.

It bounced onto the floor and broken into several pieces.

Lucian and Georgina jumped into the portal, and I followed right behind them.

We popped out right back into the maze by the owl. Lucian ran toward the path to the exit of the maze. Georgina and I were right on his heels.

"The second we're out, I'll take us into a shadow. Be ready."

We ran as quickly as we could. A few twists and turns later, I could see the exit to the maze right in front of Lucian. He ran through, then Georgina and I came out side by side. We all stopped short as another line of stone soldiers stood in our way. And right in front of them stood Athena, in all her glory.

"Stop!" she commanded. Her voice vibrated all around us.

We did. There was no denying that we were outnumbered and outgunned. We'd never be able to fight our way out of this situation. Not with Athena leading the charge. She was a fierce fighter; some would say she was even better than Ares when it came to battle.

Panicking, I surveyed the area, looking for the closest shadows to pull toward me. Maybe I could still get us out of here without having to fight.

"You will come with me," Athena said.

"Why? What did we do wrong?" I demanded, taking a step forward.

Lucian frowned at me, in warning. He hated it when I smack talked to the Gods.

"You have entered a forbidden area of the academy."

"Why is a library forbidden?" I was pushing, I knew, but I refused to go quietly.

"You can discuss that with Zeus in the detention center," she said.

"Prison cells, you mean."

Her eyes narrowed at me. "The academy doesn't have a prison."

"Right. Tell that to Jasmine, who is still in there after being tortured for something she didn't do."

Athena frowned. "I'm sure that isn't what happened."

I took another step forward. I could see that the Goddess was having doubts. She probably didn't know about what exactly, but there were obviously some things going on that she wasn't aware of. Maybe I could convince her to take a stand, to pick sides, to learn the truth.

"Were you aware that the academy was founded by Prometheus, a Titan, and a human named Hesiod?"

"Of course. We were all there when it was founded."

I frowned. Huh. I obviously wasn't as smart as I thought I was.

She waved her arms toward the stone soldiers. "Escort these three to the detention center."

The statues marched toward us, fanning out, and

coming around to the sides to flank us. We were trapped in the middle of them. I didn't see a way out of this. Lucian's gaze met mine. He was just as conflicted as I was.

A couple of the stone soldiers lowered their spears. We had no choice but to march forward or risk getting a stone spearhead through the heart. I looked around, there had to be a way out. That was when I spied a dark mist swirling around on the ground as we walked.

Before Athena could escort us into the academy through the back entrance near the training field, Hades drifted out of the darkness, as if he was out for a nightly stroll over the grounds. He looked like an eighteenth-century gentleman in his dark suit with the long tails, just like the one he wore for our impromptu trip to Nice, and silver tipped cane.

"Hello, Athena."

The Goddess immediately drew the sword holstered at her waist and stepped back into a defense position. "You have no business here, Hades."

"Yeah, I kind of do. You're making a mistake."

"These three violated the rules."

"By seeking information?" He clucked his tongue and twirled his cane. "Is that really what we're all about now? Keeping knowledge away from mortals. What happened to our enlightenment? Isn't that what the academy used to be about?"

She didn't respond, and I wondered if she was questioning the validity of what she'd been tasked to do. At least, I hoped she did. She was the Goddess of

Wisdom. Surely, she had been questioning what was going on in the academy.

"Zeus said you'd come for Melany."

"My dear brother knows I always come for what is mine." He grinned, tapping the cane on the ground with a click, click.

I didn't have time to be angry about the "mine" quip before everything erupted into chaos.

More stone soldiers appeared from every corner. Two of them carried what looked like a fisherman's net, but it wasn't made out of rope or twine, it looked to be made from thick, heavy metal. They threw it at Hades. But he was quick. He moved quicker than anyone I'd seen before.

One moment he was in front of Athena, and the next he was beside me, grabbing my hand. I knew what he was about to do.

"No, wait!"

But it was too late. We dissolved into the shadows before any of the soldiers could react.

Before I could grab Lucian and Georgina and take them with us to safety.

CHAPTER SIXTEEN

MELANY

$\mathcal{W}$e came out of the shadows and into the hall.

"We need to go back for Lucian and Gina." I whipped around, hoping to jump back into that portal, but Hades closed his hand and the black hole vanished.

"Nope. It's too dangerous."

I glared at him. "When is anything too dangerous for you?"

"I'm not talking about me." He walked into the library. I followed right on his heels. "If you go back, you'll be detained. And detained will lead to imprisoned." He stopped at the drink table and poured amber liquid into two glasses. He handed me one. "Look at poor Dionysus. He's still in one of those cells, even though they know he didn't try and poison you."

Hades tossed back the drink, then his eyes narrowed. He reached for my face. "You're hurt."

I pulled back from him and touched my cheek. Blood stained my fingertips. "Must've been a piece of rock that cut me when I smashed one of the stone soldiers."

"I'll get something to patch you up." He moved toward the door.

"Don't bother. I'll do it myself." After setting the drink back down on the table, untouched, I marched past him, out the door, then toward my bedroom.

He followed me. "I take you're still angry with me about the other night."

Not answering, I went into my room. After setting the big book onto the table by the fireplace, I went into the bathroom to wash and find a bandage if I needed one. Hades leaned up against the doorway and watched me as I wet a cloth and dabbed at the cut on my face.

I tried not to look at him, so unaffected, so cool and casual. So frustratingly sexy.

I hated that even now, maybe even more so, I reacted to him. He didn't even have to be doing anything. He just had to exist for desire to surge through my body like wildfire.

I whirled on him. "You knew there was going to be an attempt on my life. Lucian told you, and you still let me go to the ceremony." I stomped toward him and hit him in the chest with a closed fist. "You used me as bait, and I died."

He rubbed at the spot where I hit him but didn't back up. "I'm sorry you were poisoned, but I knew Lucian could bring you back. I'd given him the power to do so, and it was obvious he'd use it. He's completely in love with you."

He said that last bit as if it was a fatal flaw to love me. Maybe it was.

Chin lifted, I met his gaze but had to tamp down the urge to ask him if he loved me, too. It was a silly question, by a silly girl, who couldn't help the abundance of emotions she had swirling around for him.

I turned and went back to the sink to finish doctoring my battle wound. "Did you find out then who really tried to kill me? Since we both know it wasn't Jasmine or Dionysus. Did you get an answer worth risking my life for?"

"I have my suspicions."

"Yeah, who?"

"You won't like the answer."

I turned toward him again. "Tell me. I think I've earned an answer."

"I'm sure it was Demeter."

I gaped at him. "No way. I don't believe that. Did you see her drop the poison in the wine?"

"No, but she has a vendetta against me. She'd do anything to destroy me."

I stared at him for a long moment. "So, hurting me would destroy you?"

He made a face, probably realizing what that insinuated and that he hadn't meant to go down that path.

"It wouldn't destroy me. I mean, obviously, I don't want you to get hurt. I care what happens to you…"

"Well, isn't that nice." I tossed the cloth. Thankfully, I didn't need a bandage on the cut. It wasn't that deep. I moved to the bathroom door to leave. Hades wouldn't get out of my way, so I had to brush past him. When I did, his scent filled my nose and I suppressed an inner groan. I hated that even the smell of him sent ripples of desire through me.

He snagged my arm, forcing me to stop. "You have to know that I do care about you, Melany."

"Do I have to know? How? You don't really show it. I mean apart from our hookup–"

"You're more than a hookup." He frowned. "It's just…complicated in ways you couldn't understand."

"Oh, I'm not an idiot. I understand quite a bit actually." I pulled out of his grip. "I know that we're like thousands of years apart in basically everything. I know how much you loved Persephone and that when she left you, it devastated you. And now I know that I'm connected to Persephone, that I'm somehow her descendant."

His eyes widened at that. Either he was astonished that I knew about the connection or that I was connected. Maybe he didn't know. Shit. If he didn't know, that would've been a huge punch in the gut. I guessed I'd already put my foot in my mouth, so I might as well continue.

"I also know that Persephone is Demeter's daughter and that you blame Demeter for turning her against you. But you know what? She didn't. Persephone loved you, and she didn't leave you on her own. She was taken against her will."

He looked angry as he stormed toward me. "What did you say? How do you know this?"

Sighing, I rubbed my good cheek. "When I died, I was transported to Elysium. I met Persephone there."

He gasped under his breath, then he turned away from me. He slowly lowered himself onto my bed, mumbling to himself. "She's dead then."

"She said, dead is never really dead."

"What else did she say?"

I shook my head. "She was going to tell me something about Zeus, but I came back before she could."

He clenched his hand on his lap. "I'd long suspected Zeus had something to do with her disappearance."

"I don't know if that's what she was going to say…"

He looked up, and I saw the fury in his eyes. Flames flickered violently around like a blistering tornado. Not only could I see the rage in him, I also saw the anguish. There was a sorrow and desolation to him that I hadn't really understood before now. I felt sorry for him, and I knew he'd detest it if he ever knew that.

I moved to stand in front of him, and I reached out and gently set my hand on top of his head. I ran my fingers through his hair. At first, I thought he was going to push me away with anger, but instead he hooked me around the waist with an arm and pulled me closer. He nuzzled his head against my chest and closed his eyes.

As I stroked his head, he clung to me with a sort of desperation that broke my heart. I knew that he'd hate being so vulnerable and open with me. That it was costing him so much by exposing himself like this.

But I'd never betray him. I'd never deliberately hurt him.

Soon, he turned his face into my chest and sighed into me. His hands slid down my back to my hips. He pressed his thumbs against them, which sent a quick jolt down my legs. He tilted his head up and looked at me. The flames of anger had died in his eyes, to be replaced by a longing.

Swallowing, I dipped my head down and gently pressed my lips to his. He pulled me into him and deepened the kiss. Then he flipped me around and pushed me up onto the bed, as he crawled up beside me, his body covering mine. I wrapped my arms and legs around him and let him take what he needed from me.

A couple of hours later, Hades was asleep beside me in my bed, but I couldn't sleep. My mind was racing too fast about too much. I couldn't languish here, safely in Hades's Hall when my friends were being tortured for all I knew. It wasn't right, as they wouldn't have been in trouble if it wasn't for me.

I sat up and quietly got out of bed. I went into my closet and dressed appropriately, in full combat wear. I strapped a second knife to my leg to match the one I'd taken from Lucian. I smiled when I noticed that they looked alike.

I crept out of my room and went into the hall. I

located the shadows near the walls and pulled them to me. Once I cloaked myself, I took a step forward. Except all that happened was I walked out back into the hall again. I tried it again and got the same result. Hades had obviously shut the shadow portals, so I couldn't travel through them.

Since I couldn't leave that way, I was going to have to go the old-fashioned way. This time I was better prepared to venture out of the hall and to the River Styx.

The moment I opened the doors, I whistled with my fingers in my mouth. Seconds later, I felt the ground shake beneath my boots as a big old three-headed puppy lumbered over to me. Three tongues slicked me with saliva. It was really gross, and I wiped it off my face with the sleeve of my shirt.

"Hey, boy, I've missed you."

His tail wagged, thumping against one stone wall. It echoed off the rock, and I worried he was going to wake up Hades.

"Can you take me for a ride?"

His tail wagged even faster. I took that as an affirmative answer, and I reached up, grabbed hold of his spiked leather collar and pulled myself up onto his neck. Holding onto his ears, I steered him down the cave tunnel to the river.

When we got to the river, Charon stood on the bank waiting for us. His black cloak fluttered in the brisk cool wind that blew down the river. Cerberus pulled up short and whined. Considering the size difference, I nearly laughed at the dog's fear of the skeletal butler.

"You cannot cross the river." Charon's raspy voice carried on the wind and sent a shiver down my back.

"I need to leave, Charon. I have to get back to the academy."

"Lord Hades forbids it."

I blew out an angry breath. I was tired of being bossed around by everyone. "You know what? Lord Hades can kiss my ass." I pressed my heels into Cerberus's sides, like I would a horse, to urge him forward. He obeyed me for a change and lifted his giant paw to step forward.

All of a sudden Charon sprouted upward. He grew into a giant until his head nearly touched the cave ceiling, fifty feet above. Yelping, Cerberus jerked backward, and I nearly tumbled off his back. It was like Jack and the Beanstalk, and I was little ole Jack.

Charon was so big that we couldn't even go around him. We were effectively blocked from going anywhere but back to the hall.

"Argh! This isn't fair!"

I turned my canine mount around, and we returned to the big double doors of the hall. I slid off Cerberus. He whined and I gave his head a good scratch.

"It's not your fault, buddy."

The doors swung open, and I dragged my ass inside. Hades, dressed provocatively in a black silk robe, stood in the middle of the hall to greet me.

"I told you, you can't go back. You're too valuable. Too important."

"I'm going back somehow. I must rescue my friends. They would do it for me. I can't leave them there for Zeus or whoever to do what they want with them. It's not right."

He shook his head then rubbed his chin. "Fine." He sighed and rolled his eyes.

I went to him and hugged him tight. "You're a good man."

"Don't tell anyone. I don't want to ruin my reputation."

CHAPTER SEVENTEEN

LUCIAN

I couldn't stop pacing the cell. And that's what it was—a prison cell—despite Athena's assurances that it was just a detention room, so they could hold me until they could figure out an appropriate punishment for breaking the rules. It was all bullshit. I saw that now. I was in this cell because we uncovered the truth about the academy.

Georgina and I had been separated and put into different areas. From being down here before, I knew I was only a couple cells away from Jasmine. I'd called out to her the second the guards slammed the barred doors shut on me. But she hadn't responded and that worried me.

Maybe they'd released her, like Zeus said he would, but I wasn't confident in that. Zeus had been lying to

all of us from the very first moment we stepped
through the academy doors. Actually, it had all been
lies the moment, as children, when we were told about
the shadowboxes and the great honor it would be to be
chosen at eighteen to train as part of the Gods Army.

I didn't know how long I'd been in here, but it felt
like hours. I couldn't sit still, though. I had too much
angry energy coursing through me. I was glad that
Melany had been able to get away, even if I hated the
fact that it was Hades who saved her, and only her.
Despite that, I wouldn't be able to stand knowing that
she was in one of these cells waiting to be tortured.

After I paced enough to nearly make a divot in the
floor, I opted for some push-ups and crunches. Then I
tried my powers to see if I could use them to get out,
but like before when I was here with Melany, whatever
was in the room dampened all my abilities. I managed
some pretty useless sparks on my fingertips but that
was all.

After the sixth, seventh, eighth hour, I didn't know,
it was hard to tell time down here, I heard footsteps
coming down the tunnel. Several guards stopped at the
bars to my cell. One of them opened the door.

"Come with us," he said.

"Where?"

He didn't answer, just stared mutely at me until I
moved.

I walked out of the cell, and they surrounded me
then escorted me down the tunnel. I looked into the
other cells as we passed hoping for a glimpse of

Georgina and Jasmine to let me know they were okay. Three cells down from mine, I spied a motionless lump in the corner. The lump had red hair.

I pushed out from the guards. "Gina!" I wrapped my hands around the bars. "Gina!"

She stirred. When she lifted her head, I saw bruises and blood on her pale skin.

"What did they do to you?"

I struggled against the guards and was rewarded with a fist to the gut and the hilt of a sword to the head, which made my knees buckle. I was dragged away before she could answer.

The guards led me out of the underground prison, through a secret door. We ended up in a part of the academy I'd never seen before. The corridors were devoid of life, no art on the walls, no color on the floors. It was all very stark and sterile and utilitarian. Not at all like the vibrant parts of the academy.

I was led into a circular room with only a chair in the center. I was forced to sit, and then the guards left, shutting and locking the door behind them. After only a few minutes, the door opened again, and Zeus, Aphrodite, and Ares entered. Apollo followed behind them. I was surprised to see him here. By the look on his face, I thought he was just as confused about what was going on.

"Why am I here?" I demanded.

Zeus gave me that fatherly smile of his. "We just want to ask you some questions, that's all, Lucian."

"What did you do to Gina? I saw her face."

"Nothing that won't heal." Aphrodite waved her hand. "She's a lot stronger than she lets on."

I glared at them. "You won't get away with this."

"Get away with what, exactly?" Aphrodite titled her head to look at me. "What do you think is going on here?"

"Let's not confuse the boy." Zeus moved toward me. "Now, Lucian, what were you and Georgina and Melany looking for in the library?"

I shrugged. "Something to read. Sometimes it can get a bit boring."

Aphrodite sneered. "I know he's your favorite, Zeus, but he's obviously under her influence."

"Who told you about the library?" Zeus asked.

"I'm pretty sure it was in the academy welcome guide."

Sparks lit up in Zeus's eyes. He came around behind me and set his hand on my shoulder. I swallowed down fear.

"I know you're protecting your girlfriend Melany. I understand your motivations. Love is a very complicated thing. We're all capable of doing surprising things when we're in love."

The spot where he touched me heated as if someone had pressed a clothes iron to my skin. It grew hotter and hotter by the second, until the burn was so painful, I couldn't stand it any longer. I tried to get out of the chair, but he held me down and the burn got worse. Grimacing, I bit down on my lower lip to keep from screaming.

Zeus lifted his hand and the relief was instant. I slumped against the chair.

"I know you think she loves you back, Lucian, but she doesn't." He walked around and stopped in front of me. He had that sad fatherly look about him, like he was just giving me some sound advice and not torturing me. "She belongs to Hades. She's his whore. Everything she's doing and saying is for him. She's turning you into a traitor for him."

I looked at the other Gods while this went on. Aphrodite looked positively gleeful. Ares looked as stoic as ever. Apollo was the only one who seemed a little uncomfortable.

"What were you looking for in the library?" Zeus asked again, as he walked around me.

I hated that I flinched when he moved behind me again. "I don't know about the others, but I was looking for the new James Patterson book. I heard it was really good."

This time Zeus put both his hands on my shoulders, and a jolt of electricity surged through my body. I convulsed in the chair. The heels of my boots hammered against the floor. The pain was indescribable. I bit my tongue before I screamed.

"Zeus…" Apollo stepped forward.

The pain stopped, and I tumbled off the chair and onto the floor. I could barely catch my breath as I struggled to stop my body from shaking. Zeus reached down and grabbed me by the arm and put me back into the chair.

"This pains me dearly, son, to do this," he said. "I had high hopes for you. But I won't allow Hades or anyone to jeopardize what we've built here in the academy. We're doing good work. We're protecting the world. And Hades would see that destroyed. My brother has always been jealous of me. He's always wanted what I have." He turned toward the others and nodded at Apollo. "Help Lucian with his memory, will you?"

Apollo knelt in front of me and set his hands around my head. "It'll hurt if you fight me." He closed his eyes.

I didn't feel anything at first. Then it was like getting an ice pick in the temple. I could feel Apollo rooting around in my brain looking for something. I tried to push him out, but that just made him dig in deeper and harder. I gritted my teeth as pain seared in my head. Blood filled my mouth.

"They found a scroll about the academy," Apollo said. "The founding date and founders. Melany found a picture of her parents in a book of their time at the academy."

I could feel him reaching for my memories of what Melany had told us about what she learned from Persephone. I tried to pull away from him, but I couldn't move. It was like I was frozen to the chair, my limbs paralyzed.

"Melany spoke with Persephone in Elysium. She knows she's the one," Apollo said, then dropped his hands and stood. I slid off the chair like a puppet without strings and onto the floor again. "That's all I could find."

"Thank you, Apollo," Zeus said. "This was very helpful."

"What does that mean? Melany is the one? The one what?"

"You may leave now."

Apollo glanced down at me. "What is going on, Zeus? Why did you torture him?"

Ares stepped forward and got in Apollo's face. "He said to leave, pretty boy. I suggest you do that."

I thought for sure Apollo was going to do something, but he took a step back. Then after a last glance at me on the floor, he walked to the door, opened it and left. I was on my own, and there was nothing I could do.

"Maybe we should reschedule the strike," Ares suggested.

"Absolutely not," Aphrodite said. "Everything's been planned. Everything's in place."

Zeus stroked his beard. "Aphrodite is right. We should go ahead with the plan. If we want full destruction, we need to do it now. We can't give Hades time to coordinate a defense or warn the mortals of the ruse. We need to solidify our position as protectors of the world, so we can take control of it all."

I realized as they talked about their plans of destroying my world, and gaining more power, that I wasn't getting out of this alive.

Aphrodite peered down at me, like she was looking

at a lame pet that needed to be put down. "What do we want to do with him?"

Ares nudged me with the toe of his boot. "We could use him as a sacrifice to the kraken. Get things started."

Aphrodite shook her head. "We don't need another Perseus situation."

"We'll take him back to his cell, until we can figure out the best use of him." Zeus crouched next to me and stroked a hand over my head. "You had such potential. It's such a shame."

Aphrodite snorted. "They're a dime a dozen, Zeus. They'll be another shining golden boy in the next batch of recruits. Loyal families are piling up the tributes for a chance to get their sons in the academy. You can take your pick after we solidify our dominion over the mortals. They'll be forever grateful once we save their lives from the Titans. War is necessary to keep the peace."

The guards came into the room and yanked me to my feet. I couldn't stay on them, my legs were like jelly, so they had to drag me out and all the way back down to the cells. After they tossed me onto the ground and shut and locked the door, I crawled into the corner and propped myself up against the wall. I didn't know how I was going to do it, but I refused to die in this cell. One way or another, I was going to get out of here, get my friends, and together we would make them pay for what they'd done.

CHAPTER EIGHTEEN

MELANY

I pushed away the plate of food that the serving robot set in front of me. "I'm not hungry. We're wasting time."

"You can't save the world on an empty stomach. It's unheard of." Hades cut off another piece of the rare steak and popped it into his mouth. He happily chewed, regarding me from across the long table in the dining room.

Although he'd agreed to help me to save my friends, it was one thing after another. First, he took his sweet ass time having a shower, then getting dressed, only to be outfitted in the same thing he always wore. Then, it was a trip to the training room to collect a couple of weapons, and then it was to the dining hall to eat. Hours had passed, and I feared what Lucian, Georgina, and Jasmine had already gone through. What if I was too late to save them?

"Fine. If it will make this all go faster." I pulled the plate to me, picked up the steak with my hands and tore into it, purposely chewing like a cow with its cud. I swallowed and ripped off another piece.

Hades rolled his eyes. "Being childish isn't helpful."

"I'm not the one being a child here. You're stalling on purpose because you're jealous of Lucian. You don't want to save him."

"Jealousy is for foolish mortals." He picked up his napkin from his lap and patted his puckered mouth. "Besides that, I don't wish your…friend any ill will."

I smirked. "Yeah right. You Gods perfected jealousy into an art form. From all the stories I've read growing up and from firsthand experience, that's all you guys seem to do. You bicker and fight and plan your revenge plots against each other. You change sides and alliances as often as I change my underwear. It's exhausting, to be honest."

He laughed. It was the most honest reaction I'd ever seen from him, and it made me grin.

"My dear, no truer words have been spoken. It is exhausting." He balled up the napkin and set it on the table. He stood, pushing his chair back. "Let's go get your friends from Zeus's clutches."

We walked out into the main corridor. I was beyond ready to go. I was still dressed in my combat gear and had a dagger strapped on each leg. Hades had several knives hidden under his jacket, and one strapped to his ankle. He also carried his cane, which I found amusing.

"Why are you taking that? We're not going to a fancy dinner party."

Holding it up in his right hand, he ran his left along it, and the ends elongated until it was no longer a cane but a bo staff with sharp silver-tipped ends. His eyebrow arched sardonically as he spun the staff with his hand then did complicated overhead spins. He was just showing off to prove a point—that he may look like a gentleman all dressed up for a ball, but he was in fact a lethal weapon. And a sexy one at that.

Done showing off, he tapped the staff on the floor, and it shrunk back into the cane. "Satisfied?"

I grinned. "Yes, very."

"Good." He raised his left hand and instantly the shadows swooped across the room and enveloped us in a black cocoon. We took a few steps forward in the pitch then walked out onto one of the stone bridges in the forge.

I frowned. "What are we doing here?"

"Forming one of those alliances that affront you."

"I didn't say alliances are bad, just that you tend to make and break them rather quickly."

"What in the hell are you doing here?!" Hephaistos stomped toward us, a big hammer in his hand and a deep scowl on his haggard face.

"Access to the prisons," Hades said.

"No. Not going to happen." He pointed at me. "I told you that I wasn't getting involved."

"Sides have been drawn, Heph," Hades said. "You need to pick one."

He kept twirling the hammer in his hand. For a brief moment I thought he was going to use it on Hades or me.

"Aphrodite and Ares and Zeus are planning something awful," I said.

"They're always planning something awful."

"Your wife is a horrible person and basically wants to kill me," I said.

He sniffed. "You don't think I don't know that. Who do you think was behind *your* birthday shadowbox going missing? She convinced the Demos's to intercept it before it could ever reach you. She promised them riches beyond the imagination, which they received."

I gaped at him. I'd always wondered why I never received a shadowbox on my eighteenth birthday. I had always found it strange, and when I'd asked Sophie about it she'd been confused about it too. The Demos's though, never batted an eye over it. And why would they, when the Gods made them wealthy.

"Then do something about all of it, man. For over a thousand years, she's played you for a fool. Grow a backbone. Join us and get back at her." Hades smiled. "I promise, you will have a chance to go head to head with Ares. Prove once and for all who's the better man."

"Spoiler alert. It's you!" I said, hoping to alleviate a bit of the tension building.

Hephaistos glowered at me and grunted. Then he

stormed toward the wall where he'd shown us the door to the prison earlier, lifted his hammer and smashed it apart. The stone fell away in broken chunks to reveal the tunnel Lucian and I had gone down.

"I guess he's picked a side," Hades said with a chuckle.

Kicking away the bits of stone, we entered the dug-out tunnel. At the end, we turned right and ran abruptly into another wall where the door should have been.

"The door's gone."

Hephaistos ran his hand along the wall. "After you and Lucian came through here and wrecked the door, although I told you how to open it, I was tasked to build another wall." He seemed to have found a good spot because he backed up and lifted his hammer. "Good thing I know how to destroy them as well." He swung his hammer and broke a huge hole in the stone, big enough for us to step through.

I ran ahead of Hades and Hephaistos, anxious to find Lucian, Georgina, and Jasmine. When I came to the first cell, I wrapped my hands around the metal bars and peered into the dank and dark cage. At first, I thought it was empty, but then I spied a lump on the ground in the murky corner move slightly.

"Jasmine?"

I heard a groan.

"Jasmine? It's Mel. I'm going to get you out." I rattled the metal crossbar on the door. I had tried to melt it before and it hadn't worked, so maybe just breaking it down would work.

Hades and Hephaistos joined me at the cell. "What are you doing?" Hades asked.

"Trying to break it down."

He nudged me over and put his hands around the metal. "Together." His brow furrowed as he pushed power into his hands. Soon I could see a red glow. I added my hands to the same metal bar and concentrated on creating heat. Hephaistos got in line beside me and did the same.

At first, I didn't think it was going to work, but then the metal started to glow orange, then red. Drips of iron splattered on the ground as we melted the bars of the cage. When enough had melted, Hades and Hephaistos pried the door apart, and I ran inside to crouch next to Jasmine.

"Jas?" I stroked a hand over her head.

Slowly, she raised her head to look at me. Her face was sunk in, she looked skeletal. Her usual silky dark curls were in knots on top of her head. Her lips were cracked, flaking off as she tried to speak. Angry tears welled in my eyes, as I hooked an arm around her and pulled her to her feet. She limped against me, as I walked her out of the cell.

As a group we moved down to the next cell, which turned out to be empty, then curved around the corner and stopped when we spotted Demeter at the bars of another cell. Surprised, she whipped around, her hand going to the handle of what looked like a sickle hanging from her belt.

She frowned as she looked at me, then Hephaistos. Her frown turned into a deep scowl when her gaze locked onto Hades. "What are you doing here?"

"We could ask you the same thing," Hades said as his hand went to his jacket. I imagined he was going for one of his daggers to throw at her.

I stepped ahead, getting in between them. "We've come to rescue my friends."

"I've come for the same reason." She turned back to the cell. "Gina's in here." When we approached, she glanced at Hephaistos. "I'm surprised to see you here. You're not one to get involved."

He just grunted at her. "Neither are you."

"I never really had a reason to until now." Her gaze fixed on me for a moment, then she turned back to the cell.

I propped Jasmine up against the wall, then joined Demeter at the metal bars. Georgina got to her feet and shuffled toward us. Her face was cut up and bruised, and one eye was nearly swollen shut. It looked like someone had beat on her for hours.

I reached through the bars and grabbed her hand. "Oh, hon. I'm going to kill whoever did this to you."

She nodded. "Okay."

I nudged Demeter aside. "We can melt the bars."

But she held firm. "That'll take too long." She knelt in front of the bars, nodding to Georgina to do the same. She did. Together, they placed their hands flat on the ground. Within seconds, the floor beneath their feet began to shake. Then the earth fell away from the bars, and Demeter stood and was able to pull the whole metal lattice work out of the floor. Georgina walked out of the cell.

I hugged her. "I'm sorry I left you."

"It's okay. I'm pretty sure you didn't have a choice." Her gaze flitted over to Hades, and she gave him a lethal look.

He had the decency to look abashed and didn't crack a sarcastic comeback.

"Where's Lucian?"

"I think he's three cells down." She pointed to the right.

"Do you know where Dionysus is?" Demeter asked Georgina.

She shook her head.

"After we get the boy, we will look for him," Hephaistos said, then glared at Hades.

He rolled his eyes. "Yes, fine, we'll rescue poor Dion. I can just imagine what my brother has done to him."

As a group, we moved down to the next cell, then the next, then to Lucian's. He was already waiting at the bars. He must've heard us coming. I imagined everyone could hear us coming, and it wouldn't be long before a deluge of Trojan soldiers in red kilts and funny metal helmets came after us.

"Blue!" Lucian reached a hand through the bars. I gripped it hard in mine.

I took him in. He looked weak and broken down. There were scorch marks along the shoulders of his shirt. I immediately felt rage. I shook with it. "What did he do to you?"

"It's okay. I'll live. But hurry. I know they were planning to kill me sometime soon."

Demeter and Georgina stepped up to the bars. "Move. We'll get him out." They crouched and put their hands on the ground. A minute later, Hephaistos lifted the door and Lucian stumbled out into my arms.

He cupped my head and kissed me. It was a good kiss, a strong one. When we broke apart, I shyly glanced at Hades. He wasn't looking at us but tapping his cane on the ground.

"We need to leave before we're ambushed by guards," he said.

"Can you shadow us out of here?" I asked him.

He shook his head. "No. We'll have to go back the way we came."

"What about Dionysus?" Demeter asked.

Hades sighed then shook his head. "Hey, Dion! You here?" His shouts echoed down the stone corridor.

I glanced at him. "So much for discretion."

"We were noticed the moment we came through that wall."

Then a faint voice came back. "Get me the hell out of here. I need a Gods damn drink!"

Hades and Demeter chuckled. Hades gestured toward the way we came. "He must be down the other corridor."

As one group, we turned to go back toward the hole in the wall. But as we rounded the corner, we were met by a set of guards armed with spears and swords. And Ares standing at the front. "Well, if this isn't convenient. All the rebels in one spot. Lambs to the slaughter. Let's start with little girl blue."

With a smile that sent a shudder down my spine, he drew his sword and charged toward me.

CHAPTER NINETEEN

MELANY

*B*efore I could react, Hades jumped in front of me, his hands moving in circles to form a shield out of the shadows. Hephaistos also moved; his hammer raised. Beside him, Demeter pulled out her sickle and was already swinging it by the time Ares's sword arched toward me.

Everything seemed to happen at once.

Ares's blade sunk into the shadow shield, as he ducked under Hephaistos's hammer and kicked Demeter in the stomach. She went sailing backward and hit the wall while Hades pushed me to the side. Hephaistos spun around and swung his hammer again. This time the anvil met Ares's sword. A vibrating clang echoed through the corridor, setting my teeth on edge.

"Go!" Hephaistos said. "Get out of here! I'll deal with Ares!"

Hades led the charge toward the Trojan guards. He protracted his cane into a Bo staff, tossed it over to me, as he reached under his jacket for a couple of knives. He fired them at the guards, hitting one in the side of the neck, and another in the leg. The shock of seeing the blood and pain nearly stunned me into inaction. I'd never been in a real battle before, not against other people, but I knew it was us or them. Taking two of them out made a small hole in their line for the rest of us to go through.

I made a run for it with Lucian at my side. Hades scooped up the fallen guard's spear and tossed it to Lucian. He caught it and then used it against another guard as he advanced on us. I knocked another guard in the side with the staff, then spun it and hit him in the face.

Behind us, Georgina carried Jasmine through the line. Demeter brought up the rear. A guard charged at her, and she swung her sickle in a figure eight. The blade caught the guard in the arm and nearly severed it. Blood gushed over the floor. The sight made my stomach roil, and by the horrified look on Demeter's face, I'd guess her guts were churning as well at the carnage she created.

As we took out six of the guards, I could hear the metal clanging and grunts of effort as Hephaistos and Ares clashed. When I looked that way, I saw Ares slice the blacksmith God across the chest. Blood flowed down from his wound, staining his shirt and pants red, but it didn't slow him down and he mounted another attack. Ares blocked him and spun around. It almost looked like he was playing around.

"Gods, you're an ugly bastard," Ares taunted. "I'm surprised Aphrodite never slayed you in your sleep. I even begged her to a few times over the past millennia."

"Maybe because she was too busy in my bed to even think about it."

Good one, Hephaistos!

Yelling, Ares ran at Hephaistos, his sword overhead.

I never saw the outcome as I was pushed through the line of guards and ushered along the corridor. Once we were past the guards, most of them were injured, one or two dead I was sure, on the ground, Demeter stopped in the middle of the corridor.

"Gina. Stand with me."

Lucian took Jasmine from Georgina, then she rushed to stand next to her Goddess patron. They crouched together and put their hands flat onto the ground. Seconds later the ground began to tremble. Then, an explosive crack reverberated all around as a fissure five feet across erupted along the ground, effectively separating us from the guards.

And from Hephaistos, I sadly thought.

Hades led us forward again, Demeter bringing up the rear. When we reached the hole in the wall that led back to the forge, Demeter gestured to the other corridor branching off to the right.

"I'm going to get Dionysus."

"Be quick," Hades said. "Once we're in the forge, I can transport us to safety through the shadows. But I won't wait long. Zeus will send more soldiers. And eventually others like Apollo and Athena and Artemis. We won't stand a chance against them."

She nodded and ran down the passageway.

The rest of us stepped through the hole in the wall, down the tunnel, and out into the forge. Lucian gently set Jasmine onto the ground so she could rest. While we waited for Demeter's return, I crouched next to Jasmine and checked her injuries.

In the flicking orange light of the forge, I spied several holes in my friend's neck. I counted nine in a circle. "What did they do to you?"

She swallowed audibly before she spoke and licked her cracked lips. "Zeus asked me about you and Hades, and what you were planning. I didn't tell him anything, but then…" She shuddered, and I rubbed her back. "…the door opened, and a pretty woman walked in. I didn't recognize her from the academy. He said her name was Lamia. At first, I thought she might be like Apollo and be able to read my mind or something, but when she opened her mouth there were these needle-like teeth inside, and she bit me on the neck and all I could feel was pain. It felt like I was dying, like my life was being sucked out. I told him whatever he wanted to know." She started to cry.

I hugged her to me and rocked her in my arms. Zeus was going to pay for what he'd done. I didn't know how I was going to do it, but I vowed I would stop him from hurting anyone else.

Persephone's voice echoed in my mind…*You're the one to end the war.*

I had no idea what she meant by that, but if it was an opportunity to get back at Zeus, Aphrodite, and Ares, I'd take it.

Hades paced in front of us. "It's foolish to stay here. We should be going *now*."

Before I could respond, Demeter, holding Dionysus up, emerged from the tunnel. Out of breath, she set him down for a moment.

Hades gazed down at the poison God. "So, what did Zeus do to you?"

In answer, Dionysus bent his head and vomited wine all over the ground. The stink of it nearly had me retching. I put my hand over my nose and mouth to stop from breathing in the stench.

"Ah, the old gluttony curse." Hades shook his head. "Zeus is getting boring in his tragically old age."

Dionysus wiped his mouth. "It's a lot better in than out, that's for sure." Then he gagged again.

"Okay, time to go." Hades started pulling the shadows around us.

I jumped to my feet. "We're waiting for Hephaistos."

"There's no point. I assure you Ares ripped him apart."

"How can you be such a jerk about it? Isn't he your friend?"

"It's complicated, Melany. Aren't you the one who just gave me a lecture about the complexity and absurdity of God politics?"

"We're waiting. Five more minutes. Please?" I hated begging, but I would. Hephaistos had been an ally to me from the moment I'd arrived at the academy, and I hadn't realized how much of one until that moment. I wouldn't abandon him.

He sighed. "Fine." He turned on his heel and continued pacing around the forge and watching the tunnel.

Lucian came to my side and put his arm around me. "I knew you'd come for me."

I leaned into him and sighed. "I wished it had been sooner."

He folded me into his arms and kissed the side of my head. I relaxed into him, enjoying the way he made me feel. I reveled in it, even if it was just for a moment. For that brief time, I could imagine we were just two people who'd found each other and fallen in love. That it wasn't any more complicated than that.

Then the sound of a barrage of footsteps coming from the main entrance of the forge smacked me back into reality.

Hades's head whipped around toward the main doors. "That's our cue to leave." He raised his arms, splaying his fingers wide, and drew the darkness to him. Like a dog to its master, the shadows scudded across the room toward Hades until the forge started to fade to black.

"I'm here, you impatient ass."

Hephaistos lumbered out of the tunnel, his face bloody and bruised, his right arm hanging uselessly at his side. The gash across his chest still oozed with blood and gore. I was surprised he was still able to stand let alone walk. But walk he did, right over to Hades, scowling up a storm as usual.

I grinned.

"Now, that we're all here. One big happy family." Hades waved his arms around, swirling the shadows into a huge swirling tornado. They whipped arounds us, howling like storm clouds. The noise reached a crescendo that nearly popped my ear drums, then it all just stopped, and you could hear a pin drop. The shadows dissipated and we were now in the middle of the corridor in Hades's Hall.

"Welcome home, my Lord." Charon, dressed in his usual black flowing robe that seemed to float at his feet, bowed to Hades.

"Thank you, Charon. Make sure all the portals are slammed shut and put security measures at the River Styx."

"At once, my Lord."

Lucian, Georgina, and Jasmine were all startled to see the skeletal figure as he turned to me. He inclined his head. "Good to see you, my Lady."

"You too, buddy. Oh, Charon this is Lucian, Georgina, and Jasmine. My friends."

"Any friend of Lady Melany's is a friend of mine," Charon rasped.

I looked at our motley group and realized everyone was injured and needed tending. They also were going to need somewhere to sleep. "Do we have room for everyone?" I asked Hades.

"We'll make room." He waved a hand at the far wall, and then it moved as if on a roller. Where there had once been six rooms branching off the hall, there were now ten. He pointed to the new one just past the library. "That's the infirmary. You'll find everything you need to patch yourselves up. Charon will help you. He is an accomplished healer."

The butler inclined his head. "You humble me, my Lord. It's only because you taught me so well."

"That's true."

Dionysus threw up again, making a huge mess on the dark purple rug that rolled down the middle of the corridor. Hades grimaced. "I guess I'll have to take care of your curse for you." He gestured to Demeter. "Drag his ass into the infirmary."

In the infirmary, everyone got doctored up. Charon stitched up Hephaistos, ointments were applied to small cuts and bruises and burns in Lucian's case, and Hades removed the curse on Dionysus and he was sleeping off what was now just a horrific hangover. I helped Georgina put Jasmine to bed in one of the new rooms. She climbed in beside her. Then I sat with Lucian in his room sharing a large pepperoni pizza that Charon had specially made for me. He was the weird skeletal uncle I never knew I needed in my life. When I said as much to Lucian, he laughed so hard he nearly fell off the bed we were sitting on.

After we stopped laughing, Lucian told me everything he learned from Zeus and the other Gods. War was coming. And soon. We needed to be ready for it.

"Do you think Ren and the others are safe in the academy?" Lucian asked as we finished the last two pieces of pizza.

"I don't know. If the Titans are released, then Zeus will call the cadets to arms to fight against them under the pretense of saving the world. Ren and Diego and Mia and Rosie and Marek, and all the others will be tasked to join the fight. They'll have no choice and won't know any better."

"And what are we going to do? How can we fight against the Gods, save our friends, and keep the Titans from killing thousands? We'll be caught in the middle."

"I don't know, but we're going to have to try."

There was a knock on the doorway of the open door. We looked over to see Hades walk in. I was surprised he'd bothered to knock.

"I've come to check if either of you needed anything."

I made a face, knowing he didn't mean it and was just intruding to be a jerk. "That's kind of you."

"I know."

I shook my head at him.

Lucian rolled off the bed and approached Hades. "I wanted to thank you for coming to get me despite our differences. I appreciate it." He stuck out his hand.

I was surprised when Hades took his hand to shake but wasn't at all shocked when he tugged Lucian nice and close. "I did it for Melany." He let Lucian's hand go. "Don't get too comfortable, boy. You won't be here long." Then he strolled back to the door. He waved a hand. "Night. Better get some sleep because we have a war to get to in the morning."

I got off the bed and hugged Lucian. "I'm sorry about him."

"Don't be. It's not your fault he's an asshole."

I laughed.

"Will you stay with me?" he asked.

I nodded and we climbed onto the bed. I snuggled my back into his chest, and he wrapped his arm over me. His fingers stroked my arm, then up to my hair. I sighed as he nestled his face into my hair and kissed my head.

"I don't know what's going to happen tomorrow, but I want you to know that I love you, Blue. Always will."

I swallowed down the well of emotions that threatened to spill out. "I love you, too." And I did with all my heart. But a cold shiver of dread washed over me, as I knew I was going to have to do something that could destroy that love. But if we wanted to win the war, it was going to have to be done.

CHAPTER TWENTY

MELANY

*a*s usual, I couldn't sleep. Especially not with a million thoughts swirling in my head. So, when I knew Lucian was deep in dreamland—he mumbled a little, it was so cute—I crawled out of the bed, careful not to wake him, then returned to my room. I could pace in there without disturbing anyone.

I walked around the room going over everything that I'd learned in the past couple of days. I wasn't sure it was enough to win. There had to be something I was missing. I went over Persephone's words again and again.

You are the key. You will be the one to end the battle. You have control of all five elements, but they must be freely given to you.

Given to me by who? I shook my head. I just didn't understand.

Finally, tired out, I sat in the chair near the fire-place. I grabbed the book I'd taken from the library and opened it. Maybe it would give me some insight into the academy and the Gods, and a way to beat them.

I flipped through the pages reading more about how the academy was meant for higher learning of both demigod and mortal and not a place for war. For thousands of years, it was a place of enlightenment and fellowship. But when the Gods fell out of favor with the mortals and their temples were replaced with other places of worship, they started to lose their powers and that made them angry.

For another thousand years, the Gods tried to inte-grate themselves into the academy, but Prometheus and the other Titans didn't trust them. And after reading some of the things the Gods had done over the years, I didn't blame them. When I was younger, I'd read some fables about the Gods, stories with not so happy endings, but the reality was way worse.

Zeus was the worst of them with his punishments on mortals he thought had insulted or wronged him in some way. One story told of a mortal named Ixion, who had the unfortunate favor of being caught hitting on Hera. So, Zeus basically chained him to a burning wheel that would spin forever. I shuddered thinking about it. The cruelty of it.

It looked like there were some decades of the acad-emy's past missing, but then it seemed to jump back into the limelight right after the earthquakes of 1906 and 1908, caused by an escaped Titan. This gave rise to the New Dawn, and new temples for the Gods were built and mortals went back to worshipping them. Now, I wondered if the Titan had escaped on its own or if it had been released on purpose. Zeus had locked all the Titans and other monstrous beasts away in Tartarus. It was convenient to have all of one's foes locked away forever.

I loathed to think about what happened to Prometheus and Hesiod after Zeus and the others had taken over the academy. Although Hesiod would've been long dead by that time since he was mortal.

I shut the book. It was obvious some of the Gods weren't happy with what had happened. Hades namely. Obviously, Demeter and Dionysus and Hephaistos had their concerns. I wondered who else in the pantheon wasn't happy with Zeus's leadership and the direction he'd taken the academy. Could there be more allies out there?

Zeus had Aphrodite and Ares for sure. Hera most likely, since she was his wife, and big brother Poseidon I imagined. He most definitely hadn't been happy to see Hades show up. Jasmine said Apollo had been the one to pull her memories, and Athena had arrested us in the library. But what of Artemis and Hermes? Were they on Zeus's side?

I also thought about Heracles and Erebus. Heracles had always been kind to me, and once told me I had friends in the academy. Could he be persuaded to join our side? I also thought about Medusa. She wasn't necessarily a friend to me, but the last time I saw her in the maze, there seemed to be something there between us. And if the stories were true, she'd have a grudge against Athena, since the Goddess was the one who supposedly cursed Medusa with snakes for hair. Would it be enough to lure her over to our side?

As it was, I wasn't sure if we had enough power to overthrow Zeus.

He had the majority of the fighting Gods, along with the best demigod champions like Achilles, Bellerophon, Antiope, Helen of Troy, Enyo, and Phobos and Deimos. Mind you, we had the Furies; the three sisters were the equivalent of nine skilled fighters. And Hades, of course. I imagined I hadn't seen even a third of his powers.

But would it be enough? Would I be enough? How could I be the one to end the battle? I was one woman with limited powers. I wasn't a God. I wasn't even a demigod.

Before I could despair even further, a loud bang echoed out from the main corridor. I left my room to see what it was. Hades had also come out of his room. Charon floated out from the library.

The banging came again.

"Is someone knocking on the doors?" I asked, surprised. "Is it Cerberus?"

Hades shook his head. "No, he's in his kennel happily chewing on a couple of chimera bones."

"I will see who it is, my Lord." Charon swooped toward the doors, then vanished. I hadn't realized he could move through doors and walls. He returned a few seconds later. "Hecate wishes entrance. She and her companions had to vacate their oak tree as Ares and his cohorts were cutting them down looking for the gateway to the underworld."

By now, others had come out of their rooms. Lucian and Georgina came up behind me. Demeter leaned up against the doorway to her room.

"Shall I let her in?" Charon asked.

Hades nodded. "We need all the power we can get and Hecate is very powerful."

Charon waved his hand at the tall dark stone doors, and they slowly opened. A whoosh of wind from the cave beyond came in and blew my hair back, as a tall, willowy woman with long black hair walked in, followed by three small, bald women who seemed to glow. I could see a ball of light literally floating inside their bodies through their translucent skin.

"Thank you for the sanctuary, Hades, my darling."

They kissed each other's cheeks.

"You are always welcome, Hecate. I wish it was under different circumstances."

"As do I." Hecate's gaze flittered from one person to another, then fixed on Lucian. She smiled. "Lucian. How lovely to see you again."

I glanced at him, as his cheeks flushed red. Hmm, obviously there was a story there that I wanted to hear.

"You too." He nodded, then ducked his head.

"So it seems you are gathering an army." Hecate glided over to Demeter and the two Goddesses embraced and kissed. It looked like a chaste kiss, but I sensed it was from years of intimacy. That took me by surprise.

"Zeus has outstayed his position at the academy," Hades said.

"I don't normally bother myself with the battles of others. One is usually the same as the other, but in this I will fight by your side. I was never okay with how Zeus manipulated Persephone."

Hades's face changed as she talked about her.

"It didn't sit right with me one bit."

He inclined his head to her. "I appreciate that."

"Is Dion here?" she asked.

Demeter nodded. "He's in his room, recovering. I'll take you to see him."

Together, arms hooked, the two women strolled down the corridor, the three glowing women following close behind.

"Who else do you think would fight on our side?" I asked Hades. "Erebus? Heracles?"

"Erebus isn't much of a fighter, I'm afraid. He'll stay out of the fray, I'm sure. As for Heracles…he's always struck me as a dutiful and loyal man. He'll fight for the academy, however that plays out."

I sighed, frustration starting to settle in. I knew the others weren't quite ready to go. Jasmine had yet to wake up, but I was eager for a fight. Hades must've sensed my anxiousness because he moved in closer to me and set a hand on my shoulder. His touch energized me, as it so often did.

"I'll go do some recon topside. See if I can find out where and when."

I almost asked him if I could join him, but I knew I needed to stay here with my friends and allies to prepare.

"While I'm gone, you make sure Allecto is doing her job. She's supposed to be actively acquiring our weapons and armor."

I snorted. "As if she's going to listen to me."

"I know, but at least it will keep you busy." He gave me one of his rare sly grins that made my insides quiver, then he vanished in a haze of black mist.

"Where's he going?" Lucian asked.

"I want to say he's going to check things out, but I have a feeling he's going to go pick a fight."

Lucian, Georgina, and I went to go check on Jasmine. Out of the three of them, she seemed to have suffered the hardest at the hands of the Gods. Thankfully, she was sitting up in bed, when we came into her room.

"Hey, how are you feeling?" I asked.

"Better. Skeletor gave me some powerful tea."

I chuckled at her use of a name from Saturday morning cartoons for Charon.

She scanned the room, which looked similar to mine. "I can't believe this is where you've been for the past six months. It's like a goth five-star hotel."

"You should see the training room."

"Okay," she said with a wry smile.

Fifteen minutes later, I led them into the dojo.

Their collective eyes bugged out as they took in the wooden dummies, and ropes and obstacle course. They bugged out even more when Allecto, Tisiphone, and Megaera dropped down from the rafters where they had been perching.

"Are these guests or did you bring us lunch?" Tisiphone flapped her bat wings and licked her black lips while gawking at Lucian.

He started to back up, but Tisiphone slapped him on the shoulder. "Just kidding. We already ate."

Jasmine immediately went to the weapons wall and pulled things down to test them out. Georgina went with her.

"Where's Hades?" Allecto grunted.

"He went to do some recon—"

I was interrupted as Hades walked out from a deep shadow in the corner, a deep scowl on his face. "It has begun."

All of us gathered in the training room to arm ourselves. As we picked weapons and armor, Hades told us of what he'd seen.

"Zeus has released the cyclopes onto Pecunia."

Hephaistos perked up. "Cyclopes? Who?"

"Arges, Brontes, and Steropes."

The forge God shook his head. "Damn it. I can't believe it."

"Remember," I said, "they aren't acting on their

own. They're being controlled. I guarantee there is a golden rope around each of their necks. Cut off the cord and that should eliminate the threat."

Demeter sniffed. "Yeah, and getting close enough is going to be painful."

Hephaistos hefted his hammer. "Do what you will to Zeus and Aphrodite and Ares, but no one dare kill my friends."

"Our goal isn't to kill anyone," I said. "It's to release the monsters from Aphrodite's influence and to stop Zeus."

"Oh, is that all?" Tisiphone snorted. "Easier to just kill everyone."

"I agree," Megaera said, slapping her sister on her back.

I was about to argue again, but Hades spoke up to my surprise.

"Melany said there will be no killing. The cadets who fight for Zeus are innocent. They don't know any better. It's the Gods who fight with Zeus who will be the problem. Aphrodite and Ares are for sure complicit. The others, I'm not sure."

"So, basically," Dionysus said from his spot on the floor where he sat cross-legged and drinking, wine most likely, from a canteen. "We're going to try and make an omelet without breaking any eggs." He tipped the canteen to his lips again. "Perfect. I've already lived too many years already."

CHAPTER TWENTY-ONE

MELANY

*A*s we waited in the corridor to coordinate our arrival in Pecunia, nerves zipped through me. I had no idea how we were going to pull this off. One little thing could go wrong, and that could set off a domino effect and ruin everything and get all of us killed. Well, not the Gods. They'd survive. But the rest of us wouldn't.

I looked at Lucian who stood beside me, shuffling from one foot to the other. He looked like a golden lion, fierce and proud. He carried a sword at his waist and wore black armor, as Hades didn't have anything in any other color. Lucian made a comment about that while getting outfitted and it had made me laugh.

Demeter and Dionysus had given the four of us some energy balls, like the one Georgina had made me last year when Ren, Jasmine, and I had snuck out of the academy to find out about the earthquakes that had rocked our hometowns. I remembered it smelling like old cheese and tasting just as bad. But it had been effective and gave us super energy.

Charon had also given me a canvas bag of healing supplies, like bandages and alcohol swabs, and special healing potions and ointments. I handed it over to Georgina, as out of the four of us, she would most likely be on the ground where her power lay. She wasn't as good as flyer as the rest of us, so she needed to be where she'd be most effective.

Lucian turned his head and met my gaze. He smiled, and I felt like I wanted to cry. What if this was it? What if this was the last moment we were going to have together? I cupped him around the neck, brought his head down and kissed him long and hard until we were both breathless. After, he rested his head against my mine.

I could tell he wanted to say many things to me, but I couldn't bear to hear them. So when he opened his mouth, I put my fingers to his lips and shook my head. "Tell me later."

When I pulled back, I caught Hades watching us. I couldn't read the look on his face, and that broke my heart a little.

"I'm unsure if I can take all of us through the shadows at once," he said.

Hephaistos made a face. "I'll make my own entrance." A wall of fire erupted in front of him.

When Hades taught me how to use shadows to travel, he told me that there were other types of portals that the Gods used. Seeing it in front of me was startling and awesome. Hephaistos just went up to a hundred on my wicked cool scale.

"As will we," Demeter said, her hand on Dionysus's shoulder.

Hades nodded. "Okay, that should work—"

He was interrupted by loud scratching and an ear-piercing whine at the big doors. With a wave of his hands, the doors opened, and Cerberus lumbered in.

I laughed at the hang dog expression on all three of his faces. "Did you want to come, boy?"

His tail wagged.

I glanced at Hades. "Do you want to take him, or can I?"

He gestured to the hound. "Be my guest. I think he likes you better anyway."

I nodded to Lucian, Georgina, and Jasmine. "You guys want a ride?"

After we climbed on, securing ourselves, Hades waved his hands around drawing the darkness to him. "Be ready. We're going to be walking into a war zone." The shadows enveloped us, plunging the world into the black.

I gripped Jasmine and Georgina's hands. "I love you guys."

"We love you, too," Georgina said.

Then we bounded out into daylight. The sounds and smells of blood and death assaulted my senses.

Screams from townspeople blasted my ears as Cerberus growled from all three heads. I patted him on the side so he wouldn't react to the chaos all around. And chaos it was.

We'd come out onto one of the busiest streets in Pecunia, the one that cut through downtown. Buildings had been destroyed, powerlines lay on the street, and bodies of men, women, and children littered the parking lot in front of the shopping mall. They weren't all dead, some of them moved obviously grievously injured, but they were in immediate danger as one of the thirty-foot tall cyclopes hefted a huge chunk of cement wall over his head and was about to toss it.

The giant's limbs were stubby compared to the rest of him, and his skull was misshaped like an egg with tufts of dark hair right on top and around his chin, which I guessed was some sort of beard. He had one large multicolored eye right in the middle of his wrinkled forehead, and it was focused on the injured townsfolk on the ground.

I saw three, winged academy cadets flying his way, all armed, all ready to take the cyclops out. Unfurling my wings, I lifted into the air. I pointed to the injured people and shouted to my friends.

"Help them!"

Then like a shot, I zipped through the air toward the cyclops. The Furies were right on my tail. Before I reached the cyclops, a circle of fire erupted on the ground below me, and Hephaistos emerged from the flames, his big hammer in his hands. His eyes bugged out when he spotted the cyclops about to throw the piece of wall.

"Brontes!" he shouted. "Stop!"

Either the cyclops didn't hear him or didn't care, and he tossed the chunk of cement.

I had to veer to the right to miss being hit. Horrified, I watched as the wall segment smashed onto the ground. Luckily, I saw that Lucian, Georgina, and Jasmine had managed to get a bunch of the people onto Cerberus's back and out of the way.

I flew toward Brontes again. One of the cadets fired a couple of arrows at him. One struck him in the cheek and the other in the shoulder. Neither even caused him to react. I imagined it was like getting a tiny splinter in your finger. A bit bothersome but nothing to worry about.

As the archer lifted her bow again, I swooped toward her and saw that it was Mia under the armor. She lowered her weapon when she saw me.

"Melany!"

We clasped arms in greeting.

"Don't shoot him."

She frowned. "What? Why?"

"See that gold cord around his neck?" I pointed to it as the cyclops turned to smash another building. "He's being controlled. Someone released him from Tartarus. He didn't escape like you've been told."

I could see that she wanted to believe me, because we were friends, but it would mean going against everything she'd been told by the Gods.

"Who released him?"

"Zeus." Or Aphrodite, but I didn't have time to explain that. In my mind, Zeus was responsible for it all.

Her frown got deeper, and she shook her head. "Are you sure? I don't know…"

"It's true. This all a power play. Help me cut the cord off and you'll see. If I'm wrong, I'll help you kill him."

"Is Jasmine with you?"

I nodded and pointed to where Jasmine and the others were helping the injured. "I broke her out of the cells. Zeus tortured her for information against me."

Mia still hesitated, and I didn't have time to coddle her about it. "Go. Talk to Jasmine. I'll try and break the cord on my own." I didn't give her a chance to respond and flew away, trying to figure out how to get close enough to Brontes to cut the rope.

I didn't recognize the other two cadets trying to attack the cyclops. One of them, a girl with black hair, shot toward him, swinging her sword. She was kidding herself if she thought it was going to do any good. It would be like a paper cut to the giant. Sword first, she dove toward his chest, but Brontes swiped at her like hitting a bug, and she dropped toward the ground unconscious. I dove after her, hoping I could get to her before she hit, but I didn't make it in time, and she landed in a heap on the street. By the sickening angle her landed in, I suspected she broke both legs and an arm.

"Ow, that's got to hurt," Tisiphone said.

Megaera gave a little laugh.

"Try and stop the others from shooting at him," I said to the sisters. "But don't kill anyone."

They flew off to intercept the other flying cadets.

While I flew up toward Brontes's head again, I spotted Hephaistos down below at the cyclops's feet, swinging his hammer and yelling at him to get his attention.

"Brontes! This isn't you! Stop what you're doing!" His hammer met Brontes's big toe, smashing it flat. That most definitely got the cyclops's attention and he focused his one big eye on Hephaistos and roared.

This gave me a chance to fly around behind the giant and grab hold of the golden rope around his neck. As I neared, someone else flew up beside me. I glanced over to see Lucian as my wingman. Together, we were able to fly close enough to his neck to grab the cord. The second I had a handhold, I unsheathed one of my daggers and started to saw at the gold threads.

I cut through a few threads, while Lucian did the same. Gearing up to slice through some more, an arrow zipped by my face and sunk into the back of the cyclops's neck with a sickening thunk. Another arrow whizzed by me, narrowly missing my leg. If I hadn't have moved, it would've embedded itself in my thigh. I glanced down to see Ares nocking another arrow in his bow.

I glanced at Lucian to make sure he saw what I did.

He did and pushed off Brontes's neck to shoot down toward Ares.

"Don't! He's too strong!" But he didn't stop.

I had to get this rope off now more than ever. I grabbed hold of the cord again and started to saw at the threads. Brontes shook his head, and I nearly fell off. Then his big hand came up to his neck and swiped at me. I was able to let go of the cord, hover in the air and avoid his massive hand. Lucian returned to my side.

"What happened?" I asked.

He pointed down. "Hephaistos has it handled."

I glanced down to see the forge God swinging his big hammer at Ares.

We went back to cutting the cord. I sliced though another few threads, and the rope was starting to fray. As we continued to cut, out of the corner of my eye I spotted two more cadets attacking the cyclops. One of them was Ren.

I waved at him and yelled. "Ren!!"

His head turned our way and he frowned, then his eyes widened when he realized who it was and what we were doing. He flew over to us.

"What happened to you guys? There was a rumor that you left the academy."

"No time to explain," I said. "But don't hurt the cyclops. Help us cut off the cord. He's being controlled."

Dawning showed on Ren's face when he realized what that meant. He was there at the Demos estate when I found the remnants of a golden rope near Sophie's body. He nodded and flew in closer, but shouts and screams and loud thuds drew our attention.

Another cyclops ran into view; I didn't know his name. He was followed by several cadets flying after him in the air, shooting arrows and throwing spears and more on the ground, lagging behind because of his immense strides forward. He charged into the downtown square, swinging his arms and smashing trees and another building. I hoped that the building had been evacuated.

"What do we do?" Lucian asked.

"Let's get this rope off. Maybe Brontes can talk his brother down." Another couple of cuts and we'd be through.

"I'll attempt to get the other rope off. I'll tell the others." Then he was off, flying toward the other cyclops.

Then the sound of something mechanical in the distance drew my attention. I turned to see a helicopter approaching the scene. The chuff of the whirring blades intensified as it drew closer. On the side of the helicopter door was stenciled, *Channel 9 News*.

"Shit. That's the last thing we need."

I was about to fly over to the helicopter and tell them to get away, but Brontes swung his big arm around and hit the machine. It lurched to the side and lost control. I shot toward it. Lucian flew in beside me, but it was doing down too fast. It was going to crash.

CHAPTER TWENTY-TWO

MELANY

*B*efore the helicopter hit the ground, something black zipped by underneath us and got under it. Emerging from a cluster of shadows, Hades caught the machine before it could smash into the ground. He set it down on the street in front of the shopping mall, as the pilot powered it off.

Lucian and I flew back to Brontes who was staggering around swinging at anything he could. Blood dripped from minor cuts to his arms and legs, and he still favored his broken toe courtesy of Hephaistos and his big hammer. We swooped up around him again, but he was moving around too much for us to get a proper hold. I had enough.

I unsheathed my sword, lifted it up and swung it down at the cyclops's neck. The blade sliced though the last remaining golden threads and the rope unwound from his big neck and fell to the ground. The second it was off him, Brontes stopped moving and looked around bewildered. His big brow furrowed. His eye focused on Hephaistos on the ground.

"Hephaistos?" he said, his voice like thunder. "What's going on?"

"You're okay, my friend. You were under a spell."

Brontes swung around to his brother, who was busy pulling large oak trees from the ground and using them to swing at the cadets flying around him in the air. He managed to hit a couple of them, knocking them to the ground. Unfortunately, I thought one of them was Rosie.

"Arges!" Brontes reached for his brother. "Stop what you are doing!"

But Arges wasn't listening.

I flew in front of Brontes's face to get his attention. "Tear off the collar around his neck! It's what's controlling him!"

At first, I didn't think he heard me, but then he grabbed his brother, pulled him into a headlock, and put his hand around Arges's neck. The other cyclops struggled, stomping his feet which made the ground shake. Then I saw Brontes break the golden rope and toss it to the side. He let go of Arges, who straightened and shook his head. He looked everywhere, taking in the destruction.

He rubbed at his malformed skull. "My head hurts."

Brontes squeezed his lumpy shoulder. "We were spelled, brother."

Arges then noticed all the broken bodies and demolished buildings. He shook his head, then he collapsed onto the ground. Giant tears rolled down his doughy cheeks. "Nooooo," he moaned.

All the cadets in the air fluttered around, then gently landed on the street in front of the ruined shopping mall. They all looked at each other in question. They were just as confused of what was going on as the cyclopes.

With Lucian, I went to hover above our fellow cadets and uninjured townspeople. I saw a reporter in the mix with a camera and she aimed it at me. "These cyclopes are not our enemies. They didn't escape Tartarus. They were released and were sent here to kill and destroy."

I saw faces turn to others, frowning, brows furrowing in confusion. Murmurs spread through the group.

"Who would do that?" Diego asked.

"Zeus released them. Just as he released others last year to cause the earthquakes in Pecunia and New Haven, and the chimera to burn down Victory Park."

"How?" came another voice.

"The golden ropes around their necks controlled their actions. Those ropes were weaved from golden threads belonging to Aphrodite. She's been working with Zeus and Ares."

The murmur grew louder, along with whispers of, "She's lying." And "He would never do that."

"She's not lying," Lucian said, his voice unwavering, commanding. I looked at him and saw the leader that he'd become. "Zeus has been lying to us for our whole lives. The academy was never supposed to be used for war. It used to be a place of learning and fellowship between demigod and mortal. He's subverted it for his own lust for power."

Georgina, Jasmine, and Mia joined the group but stood apart, just near Lucian and me. Ren and Marek had also arrived and moved over beside Jasmine. A few of the Gods also flew in on white wings. Artemis and Apollo. Hermes and Athena. I wondered if they showed up to take me out on Zeus's orders. If they were, they were taking their time about it and had stopped to listen to what I had to say first.

I could see the confusion on some of the cadets' faces. A few, like Diego, had moved over to stand beside Ren and the others, obviously declaring their decision to believe what Lucian and I were telling them. Apollo and Athena also looked uncertain of what to believe.

Near them, the ground started to vibrate. A hole formed and Demeter and Dionysus emerged. Demeter held another of the golden collars. The reporter's camera swung their way.

"We were able to stop Steropes before he could destroy the dock in Calla." She raised the rope. "We took this off him, a golden cord weaved from the threads of Aphrodite's robes. Everything Melany is saying to you is true. Zeus has lost his way."

"How do we stop him?" one of the cadets in the group asked.

"You can't." I looked up as Hades slowly descended from the sky to hover next to me. "It's up to the Gods to fight."

Hermes shook his head, his hand going nervously to the bowtie around his neck. "He's too strong. And he has Aphrodite and Ares with him. I suspect Hera and Poseidon as well."

"It wouldn't be the first time we've fought each other," Hades said.

Suddenly, there were flashes of light zigzagging across the cloudless sky. The sizzle in the air lifted the hairs on my arms and on the back of my neck. I could smell the ozone in the air from the lightning. Then a colossal bolt struck the ground searing the grass and the last standing tree nearby, the crack of it reverberated off of every structure within a mile.

From within the flash of light, Zeus, Aphrodite, Ares, Hera, and Poseidon materialized.

Their appearance sent a wave of shock and awe through the crowd. I heard more than a few gasps coming from the townspeople.

"This is quite the little gathering," Zeus said, smiling.

I flew closer to him. I couldn't help myself. Fury rushed through me like wildfire. "We stopped the cyclopes from killing more people."

His grin grew brighter, but I didn't feel any warmth from it. "You're cleverer than I gave you credit, Melany Richmond. But this isn't where it stops. It's just getting started."

"It's over Zeus," Demeter said. "Why continue with the ruse?"

Hades swooped over to Zeus and landed right in front of him. "Because he wants a war, don't you, big brother? War is a great motivator for worship. He wants the mortals to bring more offerings to his temple to pray to him to protect them from the monsters." He ran his hand over the lapel of Zeus's pristine white robe. "But what does one do when the monsters are in fact the Gods themselves?"

"You were always so dramatic, Hades." Zeus raised his hand and blasted Hades with a bolt of light. It sent the dark God flying twenty feet in the air. He landed with a heavy thunk on top of abandoned car in the shopping mall parking lot.

"Hades!" I flew over to him.

Cerberus bounded into the lot as well, concerned about his master.

Zeus chuckled. "She's just as brainwashed into loving you as your last one. What was her name? Persephone, wasn't it?"

I helped Hades to his feet. His shirt was burned away and the flesh beneath it was raw and singed like a burnt steak. Cerberus tried to lick him, but he pushed his big heads away. The hound turned around and growled at Zeus, his three sets of eyes glowing red.

Then he charged at the God.

Zeus flicked his wrist and sent a bolt of lightning shooting through the air. It pierced Cerberus's chest. The hound reared up, his paws clawing at the air, then he collapsed onto his side, shrieking in pain.

I ran to Cerberus, my heart in my throat. The stench of burned hair, flesh, and blood filled my nose. I put my hands on his middle head and petted him, as he labored for breath. I wasn't sure if he was going to survive, the wound in his chest looked dire.

Hades unfurled his huge black wings and lifted into the air. A dark mist grew around him. The higher he floated the more the shadows gathered until he was a giant dark bird of prey in the sky. I could feel his anger growing. It pulsed inside me just as it pulsed in him. His darkness was part of my soul.

Everyone grew silent, eyes wide, anticipating something horrific to happen. Even the other Gods looked stunned, their gazes going from Hades to Zeus and back again. The usually stoic and smug Aphrodite looked a bit unnerved. She took a few distancing steps away from Zeus. I wasn't sure if she felt fear, but if she did, I hoped it was running through her veins like ice water.

"You have wronged me for the last time, brother," Hades snarled.

"You know your Persephone begged me to let her say goodbye to you." He shook his head sadly. "Right before I squeezed the life out of her." He raised his hand, curling it into a claw, then quickly snapped it closed. He laughed. "I'd considered doing the same to Melany, but it would've been too quick." He reached inside his robe and pulled out a curved horn. "This way will be more satisfying." He put it to his lips, Demeter and Dionysus and Apollo and Athena all cried out and ran toward him, but they couldn't reach him before he blew into it.

The sound that emanated was deep and mournful and sent a shiver of dread down my spine.

"You doomed us all, you stupid fool!" Hades shouted.

I didn't know what he meant, or why the Gods were acting so strangely, but it soon became apparent why they were so frightened. The ground began to shake.

Lucian came to my side. "Is it an earthquake?"

I didn't know, but had a feeling it wasn't something as normal as that. Something caught my eye in the distance. Squinting, I peered at the small mountain range just on the outskirts of the town. Thousands of years ago one of them had been an active volcano, but it had been dormant for just as long. Horrified, I watched as the mountain cracked open and red hot lava spewed out.

The sound it made was terrifying, like thunder, but what was more frightening was the creature that emerged from the rift in the rocks.

I'd read about the Typhon in the storybooks meant to scare little children. But seeing it in reality was a million times worse. It was impossible to tell how tall it was from this far away, but I knew it was taller than the cyclopes we'd just fought. Parts of it looked humanoid, its arms and chest, but its head was that of a dragon, and then colossal black wings unfurled from behind its wide back. Wings flapped, and it lifted into the air to reveal a long serpent body and tail. Then it swooped toward us, each flap of its massive powerful wings creating gusts of wind. The closer it got the redder its eyes glowed.

I looked around for my friends. We had to get these people out of here. I flew over to Georgina, Jasmine, and Mia. "We need to move these people out of here!"

"Can we move them through a portal?" Georgina asked.

Jasmine looked at me. "You're the only one I know who can move through shadows."

"I can do it." I turned to see Erebus approach us. "I'm not a fighter, but I can do this."

I nodded to him, then grabbed his arm before he could turn. "Could you take Cerberus with you, too? I don't know if he'll make it, but I can't bear it if—"

"I will." He rushed toward the crowd and started directing people toward the fallen hound.

When he was gone, a crowd gathered around me. Lucian, Jasmine, Georgina, Mia, Ren, Marek, Diego, Demeter, Dionysus, Hephaistos, the Furies, Hecate—all looked to me for a plan. Other cadets from the academy moved over, including Revana, and her hangers-on, Klara and Peyton. The Gods started to distance themselves from Zeus. Uncertainty was on all their faces.

Hades continued to hover nearby, his gaze on me.

"It must have a similar golden rope around its neck," I said. "That's the only way that Zeus can control it."

"How the hell are we supposed to get to it?" Mia asked. "It's impossible."

"We have to try," I said.

"We'll do it." Allecto puffed out her chest. "We don't have any fear." Her sisters nodded along with her.

I nodded to them. "Everyone else's job is to help the Furies get to its neck by whatever means necessary. It's our only hope to win."

Dionysus snorted. "Win? Girl, our only hope is to not die."

"Then that's our goal. To not die."

He laughed, then tilted the canteen he always carried to his lips and took a drink.

"Why are you in charge?" Revana shouted from just outside the circle.

I looked at her. "Do you have something to add?"

"Why don't we just fly out of here? We could go back to the academy."

That caused a ripple through the group.

"You'd leave all these people to die? To let this thing destroy our world?" I took a step toward her. "You think after it's finished ruining this part of town that its going to stop? Where does your family live, Revana? Do you think they're safe?"

She frowned, obviously not thinking about that. "The Gods will save them."

I shook my head. "You're an idiot if you think that. It's up to us. All of us together to fight this thing. Only then does this world stand a chance."

Others in the group nodded.

I gestured to Demeter. "Do you think the other Gods will help us?"

"They'll have to. When the Typhon is done here, it will move on to the academy and to Olympus." She put a hand on my shoulder. "I'll take care of it. You do what *you* need to." Then she ran over to Apollo, Artemis, Athena, and Hermes.

An image flashed in my mind. Wincing I rubbed my forehead, not quite capturing the picture.

Then I glanced over to the volcano. The Typhon was on its way. I could hear the whoosh of its wings. A rush of fear filled me, and I didn't know if I could do what I needed to. I looked at my friends—Georgina, Jasmine, Ren, Mia...Lucian. I wanted to tell each of them how much they meant to me. But there wasn't time.

I took out the energy ball in my pocket. The others did as well. We pinched them all apart and shared them with the rest of the group. The second it was in my mouth, a jolt of energy and vitality shot through me and I grinned.

I thought about making some grand speech to motivate the group, something about blood and glory, but honestly I sucked at putting words together. So, I just looked at everyone. "Let's go kick some Typhon ass."

The Furies whooped, then shot up into the air. They were always up for a good fight.

One by one, the cadets, my peers, my friends turned and ran, some flew, into battle. Only Lucian remained. He cupped my face in his hand. "Forever. That's how long I will love you. Even if I die and go to Elysium, you will always be my everything."

Gently he brushed his lips against mine, then he swooped into the air with two strokes of his beautiful red wings. He glanced at Hades. "You'll protect her?"

"Eternally."

With a final nod, Lucian ascended, sparks starting to sizzle along his fingers, others lined up in formation behind him. Out of all of us he was the most God-like. He had all the qualities that would make a great leader and mentor. When everything was said and done, I hoped Lucian would take over the academy and continue its legacy of a place of learning and fellowship.

I unfurled my wings and joined Hades in the air. Together we soared toward Zeus, who hadn't moved and was just watching, with a dreamy smile on his face, as the Typhon advanced. He turned right before we reached him, and shot a bolt of lightning from his fingers.

Hades shoved me aside just as the sizzling, jagged, fragment of light zipped between us. The tips of my hair melted from the blast of heat. After I righted myself, I shot toward him again, determined to make him pay.

"Daughter, do your duty," Zeus shouted.

Before I could aim a fire ball at him, Aphrodite stepped in front, creating a wall of beaming light as a shield. It blinded me, and I veered off to the side again. Blinking back white spots, I flew back.

Hades had formed a sword from shadow and was trading blows with Zeus and his golden staff. Both white and dark sparks burst into the air each time their weapons clashed. They seemed evenly matched. Maybe I could come up along his side with a fire ball and aid Hades's attack.

But I was stopped again when Aphrodite transformed into a giant harpy with vicious sharp bird claws. She flew in the air and dove at me with her claws first. I drew my sword and swung at her. My blade cut through one of her claws slicing it in half. Shrieking, she swooped around and came at me again. This time I instantly formed a ball of fire in my hand and threw it at her. It lit upon one of her wings and burned half the feathers off.

She dropped to the ground and turned back into her human self. Her right arm was blackened like crispy fried chicken. I smiled, knowing I'd done that even though I knew she'd heal. I created another ball of fire in my hand, readying to throw it at her, when a small cyclone of water splashed over me from the side, putting out the flames and dampening my one wing. When I landed, I spied Revana coming at me, forming another water spout in her hands.

Aphrodite grinned smugly. "You will be rewarded in Olympus, my dear Revana."

Revana threw the water at me, and I countered with a blast of fire. The attacks hit each other and produced a blast of hot steam over us both. I turned toward her, raising my sword. If she wanted a fight, I wouldn't deny her. She drew hers that was strapped on her back and ran at me.

Our steel clashed. The force of it reverberated up my arms. I stepped back, lifted my blade to the side and advanced on her. Again, our swords clanged. I spun to my left, lowered my sword, then back at her. This time I was rewarded as my blade sliced across her side. Blood spilled over the steel and ran down her leg. Wincing, her sword arm drooped and she took a couple steps back.

"I don't want to kill you, Revana," I said. "There's no point. We're in this fight together."

"I hate that you're better than me."

I shook my head. "I hate that you've been made to feel that you're less than your whole life." I remembered what I saw about her abusive homelife during Apollo's trial. "You're a fierce warrior, Revana. You are good enough."

"Fight her, you coward!" Aphrodite screamed at her.

Revana raised her sword, took a couple of shaky steps toward me, then stopped and sheathed her blade onto her back. She shook her head. "I won't."

The whole ground shook beneath us. Typhon had

landed on the ground. It opened its mouth and roared. The sound was deafening. I stumbled to the side as the pavement cracked between us, and the earth moved. Horrified, I watched as the crack widened into a crater. The ground fell away from under Revana's feet.

I screamed. "Revana!" and leapt forward, reaching out with my hand.

She tried to unfurl her wings but because of the cut in her side only one would open up. She flung out her arm toward me as she plummeted into the hole. On my knees, I stretched as far as I could…our fingers brushed.

I couldn't grab her.

I watched as she spiraled down into the hole. She hit one side of the rocky slope. She scrambled to grab hold of anything, but her fingers couldn't dig in.

Then she was gone.

CHAPTER TWENTY-THREE

MELANY

I smacked the ground with my hands. "Noooo!" I felt sick to my stomach.

I glanced up to find Aphrodite, hoping she saw what her bullshit had done, but she'd sprouted her wings and was flying away like a coward. Even Ares hadn't run away. He'd put on his armored helmet and charged toward the Typhon with his spear and shield. I was tempted to go after her, but my fight was not with her. She wasn't important right now. Zeus was my target. Taking him down would fix everything else.

But how? He was too strong. Even Hades couldn't hurt him, and he had the power of darkness behind him.

Persephone's face popped into my mind and I could hear her voice.

You are the key. You will be the one to end the battle. You have control of all five elements, but they must be freely given to you.

What five elements?

As I considered this, my peripheral caught Ren in flight, shooting water at the Typhon's open mouth as it formed a fire ball. Steam rose from between its lips and out his nose as the water cooled down the fire. Water.

Then I searched for Jasmine and spotted her hovering near the Typhon's wing trying to burn the membrane between the bones in its wings, so it wouldn't' be able to fly. Hephaistos was there helping her. Fire.

Down below, I saw Georgina with Demeter pushing up the dirt on the ground to cover the Typhon's serpent tail. I could see that they were trying to cement it to the ground, so it couldn't slither away. Earth.

Lucian flew by. He spiraled up toward the Typhon's face, doing some fancy flying to avoid the large fire balls it spewed from its mouth. Sparks flew off his hands as he formed a bolt and hurled it at the creature's eyes. Lightning.

I raised my hands in front of my face and drew the darkness into my palms. Shadow.

The five elements.

I could control them all, but only two were really strong—fire and shadow. I needed to be strong in all of them if I was doing to beat Zeus.

I unfolded my damp wing and flapped it a few times, drying it out, then I unfurled the other and shot into the air. I flew to Lucian. When he spotted me, he came to my side.

"I need your help," I said.

"Anything."

"I need you to get Ren and Jasmine and meet me down there." I pointed to a spot behind what was left of one of the stores in the mall. It was safest place I could think of at that moment.

"Okay." He took off.

I flew down to where Georgina and Demeter toiled away. They'd managed to get some of its snake tail buried under the dirt and rocks, but the Typhon was struggling and looked like it would break it at any moment.

"I need your help, Gina."

She nodded. "Okay."

I grabbed her hand and flew her over to the destroyed building. Lucian, Jasmine, and Ren all landed at the same time.

"What's going on?" Lucian asked.

"I'm going to ask something difficult from each of you. But it's the only way I know of beating Zeus and stopping all of this."

"What is it?" Jasmine had to yell over the sound of the fire balls hitting the ground nearby.

"I need your powers." I looked at each of them. "I need you to give them to me without question."

Frowning, Jasmine glanced at Ren, then Georgina. I could see the hesitation and concern in her eyes. "Will we lose the powers forever?"

I shrugged. "I don't know. Maybe. Maybe not. But I need for you to decide now. We're running out of time."

Lucian set his hand on my shoulder and gave me a small smile.

Ren placed his hand on my other shoulder.

Then Georgina did, on my back. Her gaze fixed on Jasmine.

Swallowing, and still unsure, Jasmine set her hand on my back as well.

"Thank you." I nodded to each of them, then took a deep breath. "Push your power into me."

At first, I didn't feel anything. Then it was a sharp small pinprick, like when you get a shot at the doctor's. That needle pain slowly grew into something harsh and stabbing. I could barely breathe as water, fire, earth, and lightning power surged into me. Waves and waves of it poured over me, through me, until my body felt like it was going to explode. I slammed my eyes shut as I bit down on my bottom lip until I could taste blood.

Then it stopped. Like a snap of the fingers.

I opened my eyes. All four of them were on the ground, as if they'd been shoved away. Lucian blinked up at me. "Did it work?"

"Yes," I said as I took in deep breath. "I can feel it all swirling around inside me."

Georgina placed her hand onto the ground beside her. "It must have because I can't feel the earth anymore."

They all got to their feet.

"How do we fight now?" Jasmine asked, as she flexed her fingers, probably feeling the loss of her fire power.

"We still have weapons." Lucian unsheathed his sword. "We're still warriors."

Jasmine pulled the bow off her back.

Ren pulled his blade.

Georgina patted the canvas bag at her side. "I can still heal."

"Thank you, my friends."

I unfurled my wings and lifted into the air. I could feel each element twirling around me, through every organ and muscle, making me strong and invincible.

Lucian's eyes widened. "I wish you could see yourself, Mel. You look like a fiery dark phoenix. With blue hair."

"Go kick Zeus's ass." Jasmine raised her fist into the air.

I flew up higher and over to where Hades and Zeus still battled. I glanced over my shoulder and saw my friends running back into the fight with their weapons raised. I didn't know if by taking all their power away, they were running to their doom. I had to trust that it was the right thing to do, the only thing to do, so I turned back and focused on the task at hand.

As I dove toward Zeus, he landed a powerful blow to Hades which sent him to the ground. Hades's face was bloodied and bruised. There were burns marks on his hands, and his shirt was seared in places, the flesh beneath it blackened.

Rage ignited inside at seeing him wounded and in pain. While I closed the distance between me and Zeus, I spread my arms out to the side, as fire, water, earth, lightning, and shadow glimmered around me. I saw the elements rippling over my skin in a kaleidoscope of colors. When Hades saw me, his eyes widened, then slowly his lips twitched upwards into a smile…

"This is for my parents, you son-of-a-bitch!"

Gathering everything I had, I flung my hands toward Zeus.

Several flashes of bright light erupted all around. Bolts of lightning zipped in front of me, behind me, everywhere at once. At first, I thought the power was coming from me…but it wasn't. Zeus had sent everything he had at me. I put an arm up over my head to shield my eyes from the glare so I would not be rendered blind, but I knew it was all too late. I hadn't acted quickly enough and now I was going to die.

I braced for the searing agony of being electrocuted. But it didn't come.

I lowered my arm just as Hades jumped in front of me, taking the full impact of Zeus's attack. Light pierced him through the chest, and arms, and legs. He fell like a ragdoll at my feet; I saw white current and sparks coiling around his body, from his feet to his head.

I crouched next to him, reaching for him. Sparks popped off his skin and onto mine. The pain was miniscule compared to the gut-wrenching agony I felt inside. I thought my heart was going to burst. I touched his face, careful not to cause him more pain.

"Why did you do that?" Tears rolled down my cheeks. "Why?"

He grabbed the back of my head and pulled me down to his mouth. "He's depleted. Finish him." He brushed his lips against mine, then pushed me away. Groaning, he curled into a ball, grimacing from the pain.

Zeus loomed over him. "I'm sorry, brother. It was not you I meant to kill."

Calling all the force inside of me, clutching every molecule of fury and rage and despair I possessed, I launched myself at Zeus. Before he could react and knock me away, I wrapped my arms and legs around him, squeezing him tight, and drove my power into his body.

Wailing, he thrashed about, trying to yank me off. But I held on, continuing to force every ounce of energy I had. Eventually he stopped fighting and dropped to his knees. I thought for sure I was going to crush him with the white light of my energy. Instead, I felt him start to fade into the darkness until I was holding onto nothing but air. When Zeus was gone, I quickly turned around to hold Hades to help him heal.

But I found nothing but ash.

I sunk my fingers into it, hoping that I could piece him back together grain by grain. A light breeze picked up and blew the gray soot from my hands. I collapsed onto my side, sobbing.

Through my tears, I saw that the Typhon had stopped spitting fire balls and grasping at people to crush them in its hands. It looked around in a daze, then it turned around, flew up into the air, and returned to the volcano it had erupted from.

I heard people cheering from nearby, and the happy sounds of relief and victory. Then I heard wings flapping in the air, and the sounds of feet hitting the ground. I heard voices calling my name. I rolled onto my back and looked up into familiar faces as they stared down at me.

My hands were clasped. My face touched. My hair smoothed back. I knew these things happened, but I couldn't feel them. I couldn't feel anything but a deep, gnawing black hole in my mind, body and soul.

"She saved us. She's a hero."

"Is she going to be okay?"

"I'll take her to the infirmary."

"Blue?" More touches on my face. "Blue, you're going to be okay. I'm going to make sure you're okay."

Am I? I wanted to say, but no words would come. I closed my eyes and hoped the darkness would come for me. Only then, would I ever feel whole again.

CHAPTER TWENTY-FOUR

LUCIAN

I walked down the street near the construction site of the new mall that was being built in Pecunia. It had been only a couple of months since the war that ravaged the town, but the townspeople had quickly picked up the pieces, buried their dead and moved on. I wished it had been that easy for the rest of us.

As I approached the construction office, a tall man with a receding hairline waved at me. I waved back and joined him. He shook my hand with enthusiasm.

"I'm so happy to see you, Lucian."

"You as well, Mayor Remis. How goes the rebuilding?"

"Good. Good. I wanted to let you know that when

we reopen, we'd be honored if you and your fellow protectors would attend the opening ceremony."

"We wouldn't miss it."

He smiled. "Excellent. The townspeople will be thrilled to know."

We said our goodbyes, and I unfurled my wings and took to the sky. As I soared over the town, I noticed other things being rebuilt with one noticeable exception. The temple to Zeus had been permanently torn down, the stones used to erect a memorial to the mortals who had lost their lives. I thought it was fitting, and I couldn't wait to tell Melany about it. I hoped it would bring her some solace.

It didn't take me long to fly to Cala to the underwater portal to the academy. It was the only portal to and from the academy now. All the other portals had been closed. Even the Gods couldn't just pop in and out anymore.

I landed on dock six and looked out over the bay, remembering my first encounter with Melany. I chuckled to myself picturing her out in the water floundering around looking for the portal to the academy. My hand still tingled from where I'd grabbed hers and yanked her out of the water.

Turning, I walked back along dock six and over to dock nine. I took in a deep breath and dove into the water. I kicked hard, swimming further down to the portal. It shimmered in front of me. I put my hands in and was pulled up into the spout. A few minutes later, I pulled myself up onto the rocky edge of the pool in the cave.

As I walked through the cave to the opening, I used a bit of my fire power to dry my clothes and skin. I was happy to still have that small ability, as well as some water skill. I could still fight, of course, and fly, but I still couldn't manipulate lightning. That power was gone. Chiron told me it was still possible for it to come back, but I didn't put any hope on it.

I came out of the cave and smiled when I saw the academy looming ahead. Despite of all that had happened, I still called the massive, dark-stone estate home and would for the rest of my life, which now according to the prophecies would be a very long time.

While I walked along the cobblestone path, I spotted Georgina just off to the side tending to the plants and flowers. She was on her knees digging in the dirt with her spade. I admired her for her tenacity. I knew it wasn't easy for her to have lost her earth power. She'd also lost her left arm in the battle, burned off by one of the Typhon's fire balls. Chiron had been too late to save it.

She looked up as I neared and set down the spade so she could wave at me. "Good morning."

"Morning. How's it going?"

She shrugged. "Would be better if I could tell the plants what to do."

I gave her a sympathetic smile. "Chiron says that—"

"I know what he says, but we both know its bullshit." She wiped her face with her hand, leaving streaks of dirt on her cheek.

"Demeter should be here helping you."

"She's in the hall with Hephaistos, getting those statues up finally. I think Jasmine's with them."

"Where's Mel?"

"Probably the same place she was yesterday."

I glanced at the maze in the distance, and then nodded. "I'll see you later."

"Yup." She went back to her digging.

When I entered the academy, I ran into Ren and Diego. They were busy helping Athena and Apollo with the new passageway to the Hall of Knowledge. Athena decided that all the knowledge needed to be out in the open.

I nodded to them as I passed by, and then continued on to the far wing of the academy. We had construction of our own going on. When I neared the tall golden doors, they were already open, welcoming people to come inside. I heard Hephaistos the second I crossed the threshold.

"That is not where that should go, woman."

I turned the corner to see Hephaistos and Demeter arguing over where one of the new stone benches should go. Jasmine was looking on, hands on her hips and shaking her head.

"Then move it, you big oaf." She looked over at Dionysus who was sitting on the floor, his back to one wall, sipping from his canteen. He shrugged and took another drink.

Hephaistos picked up the bench effortlessly and moved it over to the other side of the hall in between the stone statues of Marek and Rosie.

I watched as the forge God took care of the placement of the bench. He looked up at each statue to make sure they weren't blocked or impeded in any way. He'd constructed the statues to honor our dead. Revana had one as well across the hall and near a window. Melany had insisted on putting it there, claiming that Revana would enjoy the natural light. I didn't question why she was adamant about that. Something had transpired between them before Revana's death and I didn't ask. I knew it was private.

There were other statues in the newly constructed Heroes Hall of other fallen cadets. We'd lost ten people altogether and wanted to honor their sacrifice. It had also been Melany's idea to take over Aphrodite's Hall for that purpose, as the Goddess was no longer in need of it, since she was locked away with Ares in Tartarus alone, as we'd released all the Titan prisoners.

Some of them came back to the academy to resume their teaching, while others like Oceanus went to Olympus to spend eternity in comfort and bliss. Prometheus returned as head of the school, of which I was grateful, because as it was, everyone had been looking to me to take the reins. I wasn't ready for that kind of responsibility. I did agree to take Ares's place though, and take over the training of all the cadets, new and old. If there was ever another threat to the mortal world, I would be the one to lead the battle.

When the idea had first come up to carve the honorary statues for the Hall of Heroes, I'd suggested erecting one of Hades. But Melany claimed he wouldn't want that. So, I didn't press.

Jasmine came up to me. "How was your trip to Pecunia?"

"Good. They're rebuilding, slowly but moving forward. The mayor invited us to the ribbon-cutting ceremony for the new mall when it's done."

She smiled. "Cool. That'll also give me a chance to zip over to New Haven to see my family."

"Have you seen Melany today?"

She sobered a little. "No. I didn't see her at breakfast in the dining hall. I should've gone to her room to make sure she ate."

I nodded. "It's okay. Don't worry about it. I'm sure I know where she is."

The moment I stepped out the back door of the academy, I flapped my wings and shot up into the sky. Flying still gave me such a thrill. One I was sure that wouldn't ever grow old. I swooped over the garden, and the stone statues guarding the maze. I knew exactly where to go.

I slowly dropped into the middle of the maze behind a piece of hedge near the gazebo. I folded my wings behind me and then got onto the path. I spotted Melany just past one of the thick round columns sitting on one of the stone benches in the gazebo. She sort of had this glow about her now. It wasn't bright, just a soft golden aura that surrounded her. Chiron said it was because of all the conflicting energy she still had in her.

"I think they're putting up the statues in the hall today. I'm going to check it out later. I imagine it will be a sight better than all that gold and pink that Aphrodite had up on her walls." She paused, then laughed. "I know, right? Heph keeps asking me to make one of you, but I told him you'd hate that." She laughed again. "I agree. He'd never be able to capture your style." Then she paused again.

I took a step forward and saw her frown. She brought a hand up to her face and wiped at her eyes, then she whispered, "I miss you."

I couldn't stand to see her like this; it broke my heart every day. Ever since we returned to the academy, she'd been coming here to the gazebo every day. And every day I heard her talking to herself. I worried about her state of mind. Maybe taking all the powers of the Gods had broken her. Chiron had assured me that her body was healthy but he couldn't tell me anything about what went on in her head.

I continued to walk to the gazebo, making no attempt at being quiet any longer. She probably knew I was there anyway. Her head came up as I stepped up into the arbor. She smiled.

"I saw you fly in. You look good in white."

I rustled my wings a bit, one white feather stuck out and I smoothed it down. Shortly after the war, my wings had turned white. As had Georgina's, Jasmine's,

Ren's, all of those who had fought in the battle. We'd all became demigods in the end.

Except for Melany. Her wings stayed black. And I suspected she was more than a demigod. So much more.

"Did you eat today?" I asked her.

She shook her head, sending her blue hair swinging. It had grown long in the past few months but had stayed blue. Even the new hair had been tinged that color.

"You need to eat, Blue. You're getting too skinny," I teased her. She was far from skinny. Her body had grown more muscular and lean and fierce. But I worried because I didn't know what was fueling her. She hardly ate anything anymore.

She reached for me and grabbed my hand. "Are there pancakes?"

I laughed. "Yes, there are most definitely pancakes, and fruit and whipped cream, just the way you like them."

"Okay. Let's go eat some pancakes."

I pulled her to her feet and then swung an arm around her shoulders. I leaned in and kissed her. She kissed me back with more passion than she'd had in the past few months. When she pulled back, she smiled, and it was big and warm and made my heart skip a beat. Maybe she wasn't as lost as I thought she was.

We walked out of the gazebo and started for the path through the hedges. Before we turned the corner, I glanced over my shoulder at the gazebo again. Curls of black mist swirled around the other stone bench. In the exact same place I'd always seen Hades sit in the past.

I shook my head then turned back and gave Melany's shoulder a squeeze. She was going to be okay. I knew that now.

Hades had made a promise to always protect her, and he was keeping it. Eternally.

***

Thank you for reading Demigods Academy! Don't miss SEASON TWO now available! We hope you enjoyed Melany's adventures and can't wait to share more with you. In the meantime, we would love to read your opinion on Amazon and Goodreads! And be sure to join our EMAIL and SMS lists below to don't miss any of our future books!

Sign Up for EMAILS at:
www.KieraLegend.com
www.ElisaSAmore.com/Vip-List

To Sign Up for SMS:
Text AMORE to 77948
Text LEGEND to 77948

Elisa S. Amore is the number-one bestselling author of the paranormal romance saga *Touched*.

Vanity Fair Italy called her "the undisputed queen of romantic fantasy." After the success of Touched, she produced the audio version of the saga featuring Hollywood star Matt Lanter (*90210, Timeless, Star Wars*) and Disney actress Emma Galvin, narrator of *Twilight* and *Divergent*. Elisa is now a full-time writer of young adult fantasy. She's wild about pizza and also loves traveling, which she calls a source of constant inspiration. With her successful series about life and death, Heaven and Hell, she has built a loyal fanbase on social media that continues to grow, and has quickly become a favorite author for thousands of readers in the U.S.

Visit Elisa S. Amore's website and join her List of Readers at www.ElisaSAmore.com and Text AMORE to 77948 for new release alerts.

FOLLOW ELISA S. AMORE:
facebook.com/eli.amore
facebook.com/groups/amoreans
instagram.com/eli.amore
twitter.com/ElisaSAmore

elisa.amore@touchedsaga.com
***

Kiera Legend writes Urban Fantasy and Paranormal Romance stories that bite. She loves books, movies and Tv-Shows. Her best friends are usually vampires, witches, werewolves and angels. She never hangs out without her little dragon. She especially likes writing kick-ass heroines and strong world-buildings and is excited for all the books that are coming!

Text LEGEND to 77948 to don't miss any of them (US only) or sign up at www.kieralegend.com to get an email alert when her next book is out.

FOLLOW KIERA LEGEND:
facebook.com/groups/kieralegend
facebook.com/kieralegend
authorkieralegend@gmail.com

***

CPSIA information can be obtained
at www.ICGtesting.com
Printed in the USA
FSHW020014120620
71120FS